"I do want you," he said bluntly

"I thought when you kissed me back you wanted me," he went on. "I'm not asking you to rush into bed with me, Molly. Just to respond honestly to me, so I know where the hell I am with you."

The muted frustration in his voice made her squirm. "I'm sorry," she explained desperately. "I just didn't want to feel pressured."

"All right," he said after a pause. "I can understand that. But what do you expect of me now, Molly? Am I supposed to propose marriage before I'm allowed near you again?"

Put like that, her attitude did seem hopelessly unreasonable, she realized. "No..." She swallowed hard. "No. You don't have to do that."

His hand under her chin slid around to cup her cheek. "That's fine," he said, his smile encouraging. "Now we're getting somewhere!"

EMMA DARCY nearly became an actress until her fiancé declared he preferred to attend the theater *with* her. She became a wife and mother. Later she took up oil painting—unsuccessfully, she remarks. Then she tried architecture, designing the family home in New South Wales. Next came romance writing—"the hardest and most challenging of all the activities," she confesses.

Books by Emma Darcy

Don't miss any of our special offers. Write to us at the following address for information on our newest releases.

Harlequin Reader Service
901 Fuhrmann Blvd., P.O. Box 1397, Buffalo, NY 14240
Canadian address: P.O. Box 603,
Fort Erie, Ont. L2A 5X3

EMMA DARCY

woman of honour

Harlequin Books

TORONTO • NEW YORK • LONDON
AMSTERDAM • PARIS • SYDNEY • HAMBURG
STOCKHOLM • ATHENS • TOKYO • MILAN

Harlequin Presents first edition March 1987
ISBN 0-373-10960-1

Original hardcover edition published in 1986
by Mills & Boon Limited

CHAPTER ONE

'YOU are the woman I've been waiting for all my life. I love the way you talk, the way you walk, the way you toss your head.' His fingers softly raked the silk of her hair then brushed her cheek in a featherlight caress. 'I love the vivacity of your face and the quickness of your mind. You're the woman a man could wait a lifetime to meet, but I met you tonight.'

The seductive power of his words pulled at Molly's heart. Her eyes clung to the melting softness in his. She wanted to give in, ached to give in, craved for the love he was promising . . . but the panicky fear in the back of her mind demanded caution . . . demanded proof.

A wry little smile curved the sensual lips. 'I don't want the magic to end, but you don't quite believe in it, do you, Molly?'

The lump in her throat, the tight constriction in her chest, made it almost impossible to speak. 'It's . . . it's been a wonderful night,' she got out huskily.

'The first of many, my love. I'll come to Sydney soon. Be waiting for me.'

His mouth claimed hers again and she was more shaken by the gentle sweetness of this farewell salute than by the passionate kisses which had almost drawn her surrender.

Again he stroked her cheek with infinite

tenderness. 'Sweet dreams,' he murmured, slowly releasing her, back-stepping the few paces to the door as if he could hardly bear to leave, the soft brown eyes intensely scanning her face, imprinting it on his memory. Then abruptly he turned, opened the door and was gone.

In an agony of indecision Molly rushed to the doorway. Her eyes drank in the tall, retreating figure, hating each stride which took him further away. The words screamed across her mind, 'Don't go! Come back! You're the man I've been waiting for . . .' But maybe tonight had been an illusion . . . magic that would go away and leave her bereft . . . as it had done before. So her tongue remained still, and Jeremy reached the end of the hotel corridor and turned a corner, beyond recall.

Molly slumped against the door-jamb, telling herself she was all kinds of a fool. At twenty-six years of age she was too old to be retreating into virginal timidity at the first flare of desire. It had been three years, three long years since she had even felt desire for a man and she had wanted Jeremy to make love to her tonight. Really wanted him. So much that the dragging ache of frustration was a sickness inside her.

It was an effort to pull herself together and shut the door. Tears pricked her eyes as her gaze fell on the rumpled bedspread. They could have been making love now, Jeremy's arms around her, their bodies heated with pleasure and the sweet words of love in her ears. What had she gained by refusing? Only this sick emptiness. And a measure of self-respect.

Not even at twenty-six was she going to let anyone . . . not anyone . . . regard her as a one-night stand. Her chin tilted with pride. Molly Fitzgerald was no man's plaything. If Jeremy loved her, let him come after her and prove that the strong attraction they had felt tonight was more than a fleeting affair. She had been played for a fool once. Once was enough.

Her teeth gritted as the memory of Philippe slid into her mind. She had given herself to him so wholeheartedly, innocently believing that theirs was a love which transcends all others. Except Philippe was already married, and his love for his wife and children was in a separate compartment, hidden from Molly and not revealed to her until she brought up the subject of marriage. Love in Paris. A dream. Cruelly shattered.

Love in Surfers' Paradise. It was probably another dream. Wasn't that what the tourist industry sold? Come to the Queensland Gold Coast where the beaches are littered with beautiful men and women and have the holiday of a lifetime! Well, she had come, and she had met a beautiful man on the last night of her holiday, but only time would prove him to be the man who would last her a lifetime.

With a sigh which was half-longing, half-hope, Molly wandered into the small bathroom to cream off her make-up. She opened the jar of cleanser, scooped out an ample gob and was about to smear it over her skin when she paused, eyeing her reflection in the mirror and recalling Jeremy's soft words.

'The vivacity of your face . . .'

Was it vivacious? She smiled. Clear blue eyes twinkled back at her. She was reasonably happy with her face. She wished her mouth was not quite so wide. A smile made her face all smile, but at least her teeth were good. And her nose was straight. Her eyes were very good, almost violet sometimes.

'. . . The way you toss your head . . .'

Her hair was her best feature. The red-gold mane had been softly layered to give a cascade effect on to her shoulders. She tossed it experimentally and watched the thick waves ripple back into place. This was not a conscious habit with her but Jeremy's words provoked an awareness that she did toss her head occasionally. Such affectations in other people irritated her. Molly resolved to stop herself from doing it in the future. Except for Jeremy's benefit. If he loved it she would indulge him. If he turned up in her life again. When he turned up, her heart insisted.

By the time Molly was ready to occupy her lonely bed she felt more at peace with herself. She slept without dreaming and awoke next morning without any sense of regret. If Jeremy had been sincere there would be another meeting. Nothing had been spoilt. Last night had been a beginning. A wonderful beginning. There would be a better time and place for a commitment to each other, if it was love which had burst upon them in the few hours they had spent together. In a mood of buoyant anticipation Molly rose and prepared for the trip home.

The flight to Sydney passed in a dream of what had been and what could be with Jeremy

Lambert. The landing at Mascot Airport was coming down to earth in more ways than one. Molly collected her luggage and struggled over to the taxi rank. The holiday was over. Tomorrow, maybe even tonight, it would be back to business as usual. She wondered how Beth had coped in her absence.

Molly mused over the success of their joint venture as the taxi carried her through the city. Beth still had a tendency to overbook, even though they had enough regular clients to assure them of a steady and secure income. Ever since Beth's husband had run out on her, leaving behind a crippling pile of debts, she had been understandably obsessed with money; having it, saving it, never letting an opportunity slip by of making more.

Dial-A-Dinner-Party had been Molly's brain-wave. She had been working as a chef in the restaurant run by the Pattersons when the whole business fell apart with Brendan's defection. Beth had been distraught and defeated, unable to carry on with no money to meet overheads.

While the restaurant had been operating successfully, there had been quite a few customers who had requested take-aways for home dinner parties, and the requests were always for the speciality dishes which few cooks could produce without high-class training. Molly had learnt the art of cordon bleu cooking in Paris, along with the more personal and painful lessons she had learnt from Philippe Bourienne.

Beth also had a fine hand in the kitchen and with both women sharing this talent and a thorough disillusionment with love and men in general, they had pooled their resources and poured all their energies into making Dial-A-Dinner-Party the success it had become. They cooked the finest food with their own special touch of creativity, and, if their customer was prepared to pay the extra fee, they served it with style. They needed no other advertisement but word-of-mouth.

This was the first holiday Molly had taken in the two years since they had started up and it had only been possible because the business had grown lucrative enough to employ Gina Tomassetti. Beth would not take a holiday at all. Holidays were a waste of money.

The taxi pulled up outside the house they had rented at Artarmon and the cabbie helped Molly with her luggage. She was fishing in her handbag for the door-key when the door was suddenly pulled open.

'I don't believe it!' Beth grinned. 'You've actually got a Gold Coast tan. I didn't think redheads ever tanned.'

Molly laughed. 'It can be achieved with great care, much oil, and only then very lightly.'

'Good holiday?' Beth asked as she relieved Molly of a suitcase and ushered her inside.

'Really good. How's business?'

'Booming. We're booked solid for the next three weeks.'

'Just as well I'm back. Did Gina make it through all right?'

'Great! She loves the work, Molly, and she really is a tremendous asset to us. Her Italian dishes are superb. We've had lots of compliments about them.'

Molly shot Beth a look of smug triumph as they entered her bedroom.

Beth sighed a surrender. 'I know. You told me so. It's just that . . .'

'You didn't want to divide the cake into three,' Molly teased.

Beth pulled a wry grimace as she dumped the suitcase on the bed. 'OK. So I was wrong.'

Molly pressed her advantage. 'And you're wrong about not taking a holiday, too. You need a break, Beth.'

She eyed her friend critically as she opened her bags for unpacking. Beth had always been slim but now Molly noticed how thin she had become. Beth's face seemed almost gaunt, the skin stretched too tightly over the high cheekbones. The tired wrinkles around the hazel eyes did not suit a woman of twenty-nine. A tall woman needed more flesh, and with the long, brown hair scraped back into a bun there was a loss of femininity, a sharpness about her which could do with some softening.

'I should cart you off to a health farm. You'd be made to relax there,' she commented.

'Tell me all about your holiday. I'll have one by proxy,' came the unrelenting reply. Beth flopped on to the bed and raised expectant eyebrows.

Molly shot her a look of exasperation but there seemed no point in arguing and she was quite happy to relate her doings as she unpacked. 'Well, I lazed on the beach, read a few books, went sightseeing, bought some irresistible clothes, dined on inferior food . . .'

Beth chuckled appreciatively.

'. . . and, on my very last night, I met a lovely man.'

'A man!'

'Don't sound so surprised. They are around, you know,' Molly said drily.

'You've never shown much interest,' Beth frowned.

'Well, we have been rather busy these last two years.' Her eyes softened with compassion as she saw the tightness around Beth's mouth. 'They're not all like Brendan. I would like to marry some day, Beth. When I find the right man. Jeremy could be the one.'

Instantly Beth was off the bed, wringing her hands as she paced around with taut little steps, her whole body tense with worry. 'What will I do if you leave me? What will I do?'

'Stop it!' Molly blasted at her.

Beth jerked to a stop and looked at her with lost, frantic eyes.

'Stop jumping damned hurdles before you come to them! Honestly, Beth, if that little performance doesn't tell you you need a holiday, then you ought to know you're a candidate for a nervous collapse.' She sighed and dropped her voice to a calming tone. 'I'm not sure I'll marry Jeremy. We've a long way to go yet. In any case I wouldn't just run off. We've got Gina to step into my place and if necessary we'll get someone else to help, too. The business is solid, Beth. You've got nothing to worry about.'

'I'm sorry.' She ran a trembling hand across her eyes and drew in a deep breath. 'Of course you're right. I was being silly.' She dropped on to the bed again and tried an appeasing smile. 'Who is this Jeremy?'

'Jeremy Lambert. He's a salesman. He was attending a convention at the hotel where I was staying.'

'Does he live in Sydney?'

'No. Brisbane. But he's coming down in a few weeks so I hope to see him then.'

'A salesman,' Beth repeated doubtfully. 'I'm not sure I'd trust a salesman, Molly.'

It was a sad thought but Molly doubted that Beth would ever trust any man again. Brendan's betrayal had been far deeper and more devastating than Philippe's. 'Wait until you meet him,' she said brightly. 'Now you'd better tell me what work you've lined up.'

It was clear that Beth would only be discomfited if Molly kept on about Jeremy but she was glad that she had told Beth about him. By the time . . . if there came a time when Molly wanted to get out of the business, Beth might now adjust to the idea without trauma.

Gina and Beth were handling everything tonight. Molly was pleased to have the night free and even more pleased when Jeremy telephoned. Her heart pulsed with delight as he announced himself over the line.

'Where are you?' she cried excitedly.

'Too far away, my love. I miss you. I've missed you all day. Every minute of every hour of this long, empty day.'

'Oh, Jeremy,' she breathed softly. 'I thought last night might be a dream. I'm so happy you've called.'

'I can't stay away from you, Molly. It's as simple as that. I've made arrangements so that I can stay in Sydney for a week, starting on Thursday, the fourteenth. Will you be free?' His voice held love and yearning.

Molly's response was instant and eager. 'I'll see what I can arrange.'

'Well, at least you'll be free at night even if you have to work during the day. I'll be content with that.'

Molly's heart plummeted. The situation was the opposite to what Jeremy was assuming. He did not notice her hesitation.

'Nothing is too good for you, Molly. I've got it all planned. We'll have picnics on the harbour, tour all the good night-spots, dance into the morning, anything and everything you'd like to do. I want it to feel like . . . like a honeymoon. It could be good practice for the real thing.' He chuckled, and it was a happy, bubbly sound. 'I do so love you, Molly Fitzgerald. I loved you from the moment we met. I've loved you ever since. I'll love you always.'

Her head was spinning. It was too much to take in. But she could not disappoint him. Could not disappoint herself. Somehow she would manage the time off to be with him. 'You're sweeping me off my feet,' she said dizzily.

'I wish I was there to sweep you into my arms. The fourteenth, Molly. The days won't be able to go fast enough.'

'For me neither,' she sighed.

His sigh was almost a groan. 'You don't know what it's doing to me just hearing your voice. Did I tell you I love your voice, Molly? I could lie here and listen to it all night. Forever. But it's so damned frustrating not to have you with me. I won't call again until I can be with you. The fourteenth, my darling. Be waiting for me.'

'I will. Thank you so much for calling, Jeremy.'

'Good night, my love.'

'Good night,' she echoed softly.

Molly sat in a daze conjuring up Jeremy's image in her mind; the devil-may-care smile which had first attracted her attention, the dancing brown eyes and crisp black hair, the whole, handsome, clean-cut look of him. He really was a lovely man in every way. And he made her feel so very special.

The fourteenth. Only ten days away. If she did all the dinner parties between now and then, and took over all the food-buying while Jeremy was here . . . He might even like to help her with that. It would probably be an eye-opening experience for him and surely it would be fun, just being together. She was sure that Beth and Gina would not mind. It was only for a week.

When Molly broached the subject the next morning both women readily agreed to her plan, with Beth keeping whatever thoughts she had carefully reserved and Gina volubly expressing herself on love affairs in general. She was a plump, happy woman who found excitement in all manner of things, her very Italian face lighting up, hands gesticulating wildly and the profusion of black curls on her head bobbing an accompaniment to every burst of words. She made Molly, and even Beth, smile.

On checking the bookings for the coming days, Molly discovered a dinner party to be personally served on Sunday night. She confronted Beth with some asperity. Money-grubbing could be taken too far. 'I thought we agreed on leaving Sundays free.'

'Don't take that tone, Molly. I only did it for your sake. You're the ballet nut.'

'What's ballet got to do with it?'

Beth's smile was distinctly smug. 'The lady who booked the party only happens to be the prima ballerina of the ballet company. That's her married name there, but she's Anita Daniels, who happens to be dancing the lead role in that *Lyre Bird* thing you raved on about when you read it was to be revived this season. And since she proceeded to bribe me with the promise of two free tickets if we relaxed our rule and did the dinner party for her . . .'

'Free tickets!' Molly squeaked and rushed upon Beth to hug her excitedly. 'Oh, you angel! Those tickets are pure gold.'

'So now you can apologise,' said Beth, an affectionate indulgence overriding the attempt at haughty disdain.

'I apologise. I apologise. You're the best businesswoman I know,' Molly crowed in delight. 'Come to the ballet with me. We'll take the night off. You'll love it, Beth.'

'Now you're going too far. You know ballet's

not my thing, and I've told you we're booked solid for the next three weeks. That means only one of us off. Maybe the tickets will be for a night when Jeremy's here and you can take him.'

It was a thrill for Molly to actually meet Anita Daniels, but when she was given tickets to the actual première of the ballet, which was on the night of the fourteenth, she could hardly contain her excitement. She hoped Jeremy was as keen on ballet as she was, but even if he wasn't he would enjoy seeing *The Lyre Bird*. It had won tremendous acclaim wherever it had been danced, except in Paris where the matrons had walked out in disgust at its highly erotic theme. Molly grinned to herself. Jeremy would surely be amused to hear that. And it would arouse his curiosity and interest. The men in Paris had stayed glued to their seats.

The fourteenth finally arrived. Molly was floating on a cloud of happiness from the moment her eyes opened on a beautiful sunny morning. By mid-afternoon a shadow of anxiety was clipping back some of her joy. Jeremy was coming, she kept insisting to herself. He would have let her know otherwise. When the telephone rang at four o'clock she pounced on it. So tense did she feel that she had to force a warm politeness into her voice.

'Dial-A-Dinner-Party at your service.'

'Molly, I'm here. I'm here at last and I'll be with you as fast as I can change clothes and grab a taxi.'

Relief and excitement lifted her heart. 'Oh, Jeremy! It's so good to hear you. Where are you?'

'I've just got into my motel room. Right in the heart of the city. Be ready for me. I'll be there to collect you in . . . oh, say half an hour.'

'No. I mean I don't want to be collected. I want you to come here. I've got dinner all prepared and tickets for the ballet tonight.'

'Ballet!'

The sharp tone and the pause afterwards squeezed Molly's heart. 'It's . . . it's a famous production. Sir Robert Helpman's *Lyre Bird*. I'm sure you'll like it, Jeremy.'

Still there was a silence, then a rush of explanation. 'Sorry, darling. It's just that I was supposed to drop in on a business associate tonight and I was wondering how to get round it. I hadn't counted on your having a fixed plan like a show. Give me some time. I'll try to contact the guy and see if I can organise another meeting. OK?'

'Yes. Yes, of course. I'm sorry. I didn't realise . . .'

'Heh!' The soft interruption purred in her ear. 'I love you. Making you happy is my pleasure. I'll call you back soon.'

For twenty long minutes Molly was on tenterhooks, holding disappointment at bay and reassuring herself that, even if she had to miss the ballet, Jeremy's company would more than make up for it. She held her breath when his call came.

'Everything's fine. We're off to the ballet.'

'That's great!' Molly exulted, then, in case it had sounded as if she'd placed too much importance on it, added quickly, 'I hope it was no trouble to you, Jeremy.'

'Darling Molly, I'd go to any trouble for you. But I'd better warn you I haven't a dinner-jacket with me.'

The dark grey lounge-suit which Jeremy wore made him look devastatingly handsome. And when he took her in his arms and kissed her Molly knew that the last night of her holiday had been no dream. The same magnetic attraction was there. Her pulse galloped with the same wild excitement. And everything was beautiful.

Jeremy had brought a bottle of champagne to drink with the dinner she had prepared, but neither of them really tasted anything despite the fact that they ate and drank. Champagne was already fizzing in their blood and the love in their eyes was the only food they really wanted. Every touch, every caress, every kiss stirred a hunger for more.

When the time came for them to leave for the ballet, Molly hardly cared if she saw it or not, but they went. She parked her car near Circular Quay and their walk to the Opera House was pure romance with the sparkling lights of the harbour around them and the star-filled sky above.

And when they were settled in the magnificent main hall of the Opera House and the lights darkened and Jeremy's hand squeezed hers possessively, Molly thought she could feel no more happiness than this. Yet no sooner had the ballet begun than she was captivated by the drama on stage.

Against the dark, brooding backdrops of the forest, the dancers played out a picnic which was going hectically wrong, the men growing wilder and out of control as they drank and heckled each other, the girls relishing the excitement yet fearful. The build-up of violence which led to the gang-rape of the one terrified victim was so powerfully transmitted by the dance that the whole audience tensed and held its breath in horror until the act was over and the girl was left abandoned, bruised in body and broken in spirit.

The solo dance which followed was one of haunting emotion; shame, despair, a terrible aloneness, then fear as the lyre bird made his entrance, and mesmerising wonder as he fanned the magnificent, jewel-like tail. It shimmered and swayed, opening and closing, tantalising, spellbinding as he began his hypnotic mating dance. Here was the ultimate seduction of nature, as old as time itself, and the primeval quality of the forest sprang alive, closing in on the girl, inviting submission, willing her to become one with it.

To the girl who had been savaged by her own society the call was overwhelmingly strong. The inevitability of the last scene was heart-wrenching. She lay on the stage in her white dress like a sacrificial offering to fate. The lyre bird knelt over her, his outspread tail quivering in ecstatic triumph. As he swooped downwards so did the tail, cloaking both figures in climactic finality.

'My God!' Jeremy breathed beside her as the curtains closed. Molly was so choked by emotion she could say nothing and indeed, so stunning had been the impact of that last scene that it was some moments before the audience started clapping. Then the applause was thunderous, demanding curtain-call after curtain-call.

The lights finally came on to signal the interval and Molly turned to Jeremy with a smile. 'You liked it?'

He shook his head. 'Like is hardly the word. Breath-taking, mind-jolting, and unbelievably erotic.' He grinned. 'Don't ask me to get up yet. I'm still so damned excited I'm likely to make an exhibition of myself.'

Molly laughed but desire was racing through her own veins and when their eyes caught and held, she knew there would be no turning away tonight.

Jeremy was not the only person disinclined to move. The whole audience seemed caught in thrall by what they had just experienced. Only gradually did the general exodus begin and gather momentum. The hall had half emptied when Jeremy led Molly out to the observation lounge. He left her near one of the windows which overlooked the harbour and went to the bar for drinks.

Molly's gaze drifted aimlessly around the milling crowd. A première invariably brought out the best dressing in Sydney. Molly herself had worn a white crêpe dress which was very elegant with its cowl neckline and softly flowing skirt, but her eyes rested enviously on several gowns which Molly's pocket could never reach.

Her eyes suddenly caught other eyes; cold, hostile, contemptuous eyes. The stare was so sharp and venomous that Molly almost cringed away from it. Pride stiffened her spine. Who did that man think he was, looking at her like that? Or whom did he think she was? Was it a case of mistaken identity? Molly was sure she had never laid eyes on him before. She would remember such a man.

She frowned at him and he turned his head away. He was with a group of people who were all expensively dressed. Molly actually recogised one of the women, a guest at a dinner party which she and Beth had done a month or so ago. Maybe the woman had recognised Molly and pointed her out. But that didn't explain why the man should look so hostile.

Molly eyed him resentfully. He was quite an impressive figure of a man, tall and broad-shouldered. The lofty carriage of his head suggested authority and arrogance. A few sprinkles of grey in the dark hair put his age in the thirties even though his face had seemed unlined. There had been nothing soft on that face. Its features had been strong and hard, from the distinctive black eyebrows to a jawline that looked as if it had been carved out of granite. A convulsive shiver ran over Molly's skin. He looked like a man who could be very cruel.

She caught sight of Jeremy heading back towards her with glasses of champagne. Molly shrugged off the disquieting incident and smiled at him. Jeremy was tall, dark and handsome, too, but his face reflected good humour, from the laughter-lines around his eyes to the mouth which could dazzle her with a smile and melt her bones with a kiss. Her heart lifted once more with happiness. She loved Jeremy. She was sure of it.

He handed her a glass and clinked it with his. 'To us, my lovely Molly.'

'To us,' she echoed softly.

'I didn't expect to see you here, Jeremy.'

The voice had the hardness of steel and the cutting edge of a carving-knife. It was the man who had stared so rudely at Molly. Champagne tipped from Jeremy's glass as he swung around, shock stiffening his face.

'Richard! What the devil? You said you had a dinner engagement.'

They were grey, those cold eyes. As grey as a sky dripping sleet. 'So I did. I was not aware that you required me to detail my whole evening.' The firm lips curled. 'Undoubtedly you wouldn't be here if I had. Will you introduce me to your . . . companion?' The mouth curled even more on that word, giving it a derisive tone.

A strong antagonism flared within Molly. Clearly this man's intrusion was as unwelcome to Jeremy as it was to her. Jeremy's neck was going red and there was something distinctly guilty in his expression. The sharp thought came to her that perhaps this intruder was the business associate Jeremy was to have met tonight. Had Jeremy lied to him and now been caught out in the lie? If he had done something wrong it had been for her sake, so Molly decided to back him up whatever he said.

'Richard, this is not what you think,' Jeremy began, definitely flustered.

The hard face remained impassive but the voice took on a silky edge. 'Isn't it? Then introduce me.'

Jeremy's eyes didn't quite meet Molly's. 'Miss Fitzgerald, Richard Pembroke,' he said flatly.

'How do you do, Miss Fitzgerald?' No hand was offered. 'I'm Jeremy's brother-in-law. He's married to my sister and, since they live in Brisbane, I'd like to hear some news of her. Jeremy was in a hurry when he telephoned me this afternoon so I didn't get much of a chance to speak to him. How is Dana, Jeremy?'

'Very well.'

'And the children? Little Steven and Tracy?'

'Fine.'

'Oh, that's good. That's good to hear. Well, I hope you both enjoy the second half of the ballet programme. It was ... enlightening ... meeting you, Miss Fitzgerald. Don't you think it's a shame they have no-fault divorces these days? The guilty receive no punishment. No punishment at all. It really does offend my sense of justice. There's something so satisfying about naming names. Goodbye, Miss Fitzgerald. Jeremy.'

CHAPTER TWO

INSIDE Molly was a frozen wasteland. Her heart, mind and soul beat piteously against the bitter realities and there swirled around her a barrenness which held no promise of life. Ever. She was locked into an endless cycle of futility. Alone. If at that moment a lyre bird had offered her escape, Molly would have succumbed to the lure of another world, because this one she inhabited offered only pain.

Jeremy was speaking but the words did not reach her. She was too numb to hear. His face was working with passionate intensity but it meant nothing to her. Nothing at all. She wouldn't let it. Jeremy was locked out of her life now. He belonged to someone else. Always had. He hadn't really existed in her world at all. He had been a mirage. Just like Philippe. Lies and deception. One more ride around the wilderness.

She turned away from him. Her eyes were quite sightless until they fell on the judge who had condemned her. He stood at the edge of his social group, smiling at the woman next to him. A rage erupted inside Molly, a wild, spurting, uncontrollable rage. That man who stood there smiling had labelled her an adulteress. The eyes which were now crinkling softly at another woman had poured contempt on Molly. And she was innocent. Innocent.

It was bad enough that two men had cheated her, promising love when they knew there would be no true fulfilment of that promise. But for a man who did not know her to have cast such vicious stones at her and then to walk away and smile . . . that could not be borne.

The stones he had cast burnt into Molly's mind and spawned the stones of a counter-attack. Her feet moved unerringly to its target. She steadied herself, knowing there could only be one retaliatory burst and the rage demanded that it hit him square on.

'Mr Pembroke . . .'

He swung around, one eyebrow lifted in enquiry. His eyes showed a flicker of surprise but Molly gave him no time to speak. Her eyes flared their venom as acid poured from her tongue.

'. . . I shall not demand an apology from you. It would be meaningless coming from a man whose sense of justice is so warped by self-righteousness. Besides which, I am quite sure that a man who leaps so confidently to hasty conclusions, who takes so much relish in false assumptions, could never consider himself wrong, no matter how wrong he is. However, since you're so very fond of your sister, may I suggest you solder a wedding ring on the third finger of her husband's left hand, or put some other recognisable brand on him which publicly stamps him as her property.'

She paused for breath. Molly was unaware of the silence which had fallen. Nor did she see the ring of stunned faces in their immediate vicinity. She saw only Richard Pembroke's face and its taut lines of shock gave her savage satisfaction. She lifted her chin and resumed her attack.

'Next time you set yourself up as judge, jury and prosecutor, Mr God-almighty Pembroke, may I suggest you check your facts first, and perhaps your sense of justice could be sharpened up enough so that you can put aside your male prejudice which condones men and condemns women. If you're big enough to manage all that, Mr Pembroke, then place the blame where it rests, and don't overlook your own doorstep.'

A muscle along his jawline flinched and Molly knew that at least one of her stones had hit. She could go now. Honour had been avenged. She threw his own words back at him.

'I hope you enjoy the second half of the ballet programme. I'm afraid you've ruined it for me. I could not bring myself to sit in the same hall with the likes of you and your brother-in-law. It was ... enlightening ... meeting you, Mr Pembroke, but I sincerely hope we never meet again. To say it was a pleasure would be the grossest lie.'

With a disdainful toss of the head Molly turned on her heel and marched away. She did not have to pick her way through the crowd. People moved out of her path.

A hand gripped her elbow, fingers biting into her skin. 'What on earth possessed you to make such a scene!' Jeremy hissed.

Without deliberation, without any thought at all ... still consumed with rage ... Molly swung her free arm around and hit Jeremy's face with an open-handed slap which had the explosive crack of a gun-shot. He reeled back from her, his hand to his cheek, his knees seming to buckle. Molly stood there with all the fierce pride of a Valkyrie and glared her contempt at him.

'Don't you touch me! Don't you speak to me! Don't you ever come near me again!' She grated out the words through clenched teeth, but each one had a cutting precision which sliced into the silence around her, bitterly clear to any listener.

Then with the dignity of a queen Molly trod her lonely path, unaware of the buzz of talk behind her, unaware of eyes following her, unaware of anything but the path ahead, out of the Opera House, down the long flights of steps, along the walkway to Circular Quay. Her feet automatically made their way to where the car was parked. She drove home by instinct, performing the mechanics with meticulous care but her mind not even registering what she was doing or where she was going.

Once inside her bedroom she undressed, hung her good white dress in the wardrobe, pulled on her nightie, switched off the light and got into bed. She lay on her back, staring into the darkness, her body completely still, corpse-like.

I don't care. I don't care. I don't care about anything, her mind recited with silent force. But the hurt and humiliation could not be entirely repressed. Tears oozed out of the corners of her eyes and, however hard she blinked, they kept pushing out in a steady trickle. And the 'I don't care' slowly changed to a 'why me?'

What had she ever done to deserve such misery? She had never knowingly deceived or hurt anyone. Until tonight. She had meant to hurt Richard Pembroke, but he had struck first. And Jeremy had earned that slap with all his talk of undying love. How could he have said and done those things to her when he had a wife and children? How could this happen to her again? Surely Fate had been mean enough in placing her in the path of Philippe Bourienne. Was she always destined to fall in love with married men?

She shivered as she remembered the cold grey eyes of Richard Pembroke sweeping her with scorn. That was the unfairest cut of all. She was the victim and he had blamed her for the crime which had been committed against her. She was glad she had jolted him out of his smug righteousness, even if it had only been for a minute. He was no better than Jeremy or Philippe.

In bitter despair, Molly wondered if any man could be trusted with her heart. Maybe Beth was right. Even given the commitment of marriage, trust could not be taken for granted. Jeremy's wife and Philippe's wife probably still believed they had their husbands' love, just as Beth had believed she had Brendan's.

Molly wanted a man who loved her so much there would be no question of any other woman even capturing a corner of his heart. Total commitment. Nothing less would ever satisfy her and she wanted her man to feel the same way, if she ever found a man who was free of any other commitment.

The trickle of tears suddenly welled into a flood and Molly turned her head into the pillow and cried herself to sleep.

CHAPTER THREE

THE morning seemed very grey. The memory of Richard Pembroke's eyes flashed into Molly's mind and she drove it out. That was all behind her. She felt completely washed out, but the early trip to the markets lent her some purpose in life. She picked out and purchased the best of the fruit and vegetables and was ready to face Beth and Gina by the time she returned home.

'How was the ballet last night?' Beth asked as she helped unpack the parcels.

'And Jeremy?' Gina bubbled. 'Was it all very romantic?'

Molly kept on loading goods into the refrigerator. 'The ballet was great but the evening was a disaster. No more Jeremy. He's married,' she stated flatly, then gave the two women a direct gaze. 'There's no reason why we can't get straight back on to our normal schedule of work. I don't need any time off at all.'

Gina looked scandalised. 'Married! Oh, the . . .'

'Save it, Gina!' Beth ordered quietly. 'I don't think Molly wants to talk about it.' Her eyes held Molly's, showing a depth of understanding which only a similar experience could give. 'Right, Molly?'

She nodded and gave a wry smile. 'All swept

under the mat where it belongs. Let's get to work.'

It was good to be busy. Molly ruthlessly cut Jeremy out of her thoughts every time he crept into them. Beth was especially bright and cheerful. Molly wondered with some irony if it was a relief to her friend that Jeremy no longer posed a threat to their business partnership, but then she understood more fully what the business meant to Beth. It was a mainstay in their lives, giving them a sense of purpose and achievement, as well as the knowledge that they could make their own way, independent of men.

A few days after the night of the ballet, Beth greeted Molly's return home from the markets with an especially big grin. 'We've got a new customer. Party for ten with personal service. House is at St Ives. Want to go over and case the place?'

When personal service was requested they needed to know what facilities were available in the kitchen, and the layout of the entertainment areas. An interview with the host or hostess was also necessary. The menu had to be agreed upon and sometimes the food had to complement particular wines which would be served. The timing of the meal had to be settled upon, especially since some courses might need last-minute preparation. Usually the hostess wanted one or two show-piece serving-dishes to be used. All such details were checked and written down by Beth or Molly to ensure that the dinner-party would be as successful as they could make it.

Usually Molly enjoyed this part of the job. The

houses and possessions of the people who could afford this kind of service never ceased to amaze her. There were many people of great wealth in Sydney and that wealth was expended in many and varied ways. Today, however, Molly was not in the mood for meeting strangers.

'You do it, Beth. Who was the reference?' she added carelessly.

All new clients had to give a reference. Beth and Molly took no risks. Beth glanced down at her notebook. 'It's bona fide all right. Mrs Fotherby vouched for them. Remember that last party we served before you went on holiday? She was the hostess there.'

Fotherby. Molly remembered all right. She also remembered the woman who had stood next to Richard Pembroke in the observation lounge of the Opera House. Molly was quite sure that the same woman had been at the Fotherby party. She frowned.

'Something wrong?' Beth queried.

It was on the tip of Molly's tongue to tell Beth to cancel the booking but she quelled the impulse. That would mean telling Beth what had happened at the ballet and she did not want to do that. Besides, there had been several other women at the Fotherby party. The new client was not necessarily the same person. Even if it was, Molly told herself she did not care what the woman thought of her. Business was business and a party for ten was good business.

Molly tossed her head and smiled at Beth. 'Nothing wrong. Go ahead. When's the party for?'

'Two weeks on Saturday. And she wants the lot . . . hors d'oeuvres, soup, entrée, main course, cheese board, dessert, coffee and nibbles. Big fee for us.'

Molly raised her eyesbrows. 'What's the name?'

'Roysten. Ring a bell? They must be rolling in money.'

'No bell. Make sure she knows it's cash on the nail. No credit cards or cheques.'

Beth grinned. 'Do you think I'd let that little matter slip by me?'

Molly laughed and shook her head. 'Go and nail her down to everything.'

However, Molly was not quite as carefree as she wanted to be. The thought of Mrs Roysten niggled at her over the next two weeks. It would be a rotten coincidence if it was the same woman who had been with Richard Pembroke. Would she recognise Molly? Had she recognised Molly at the ballet? Had she connected Molly with Dial-A-Dinner-Party?

Much as Molly tried to assure herself that women like Mrs Roysten did not notice people who served them, she had to admit that no one who had closely witnessed that scene at the ballet was likely to forget the woman who had accosted Richard Pembroke. All Molly could do for her peace of mind was hope that Mrs Roysten had not been at the ballet that night.

She said nothing to Beth about her disquiet. After all, it was a very personal matter which had nothing to do with business. The Saturday arrived. As usual they did all the preparation for the dinner party at home. They loaded the van with everything they needed and at five o'clock they washed and changed into their black dresses.

Black did not really suit Beth but she had insisted that it be their uniform, discreet, unobjectionable, and classy. The dresses were high-necked with a soft, blouson bodice and straight skirt, conservative in style but elegant in their simplicity. The plainness of the dress served to accentuate Molly's curvaceous figure and the black highlighted her colouring. While Beth looked as unobtrusive as a shadow, Molly had the attraction of a flame, but neither woman gave consideration to her appearance except to look neat and tidy.

Beth took the wheel of the van since she knew the location of the Roysten house in St Ives. Molly had made a deliberate point of not showing any extra interest in this client, determined to think of this job as a job like any other, but as they neared their destination an increasing sense of trepidation forced a question to her tongue.

'What's she like, this Roysten woman?'

Beth threw her a dry smile. 'Very upper-crust. Or thinks she is. Full of airs and graces and very sweetly patronising.' She gave a short laugh. 'I remember reading about a man who came into an inheritance and he spent the lot on old cars which he used to crash into every Rolls Royce he sighted. You know, I bet that man had been in service and he'd had a stomachful of upper-crust condescension.'

'Probably,' Molly agreed on a sigh. She was

none the wiser about Mrs Roysten, so she tried again. 'I really meant you to tell me what she looked like. Is she old, young, blond, brunette, slim, stout . . .'

'Blonde, tall and slim. Looks to be in her thirties but could be older. Women in that wealth-bracket can afford to be well-preserved.' Beth slanted her a grin. 'She asked after you.'

A chill ran through Molly's veins. 'After me?' she repeated on a forced note of incredulity.

Beth's grin grew wider. 'The red-haired girl. She remembered you from the Fotherbys'.'

And from the ballet? Ice clutched at Molly's heart. The description of Mrs Roysten certainly fitted the woman at the Opera House. 'What did she say?'

'Oh, just wanted to know if you'd be with me. She asked who would be doing the serving and I told her we worked that out between ourselves, depending on what was cooking in the kitchen.'

That seemed an ordinary enough question but Molly's nerves were still twanging. 'Did she say anything else about me?'

Beth glanced her surprise at the tense note in Molly's voice. 'No. Unless you count her raving on about how marvellous the food had been at the Fotherbys' party; so I guess you can consider yourself complimented.'

Molly's tension eased. 'Well, it's always nice to know one's work is appreciated.'

'Mmm. Words are cheap. A tip's better.'

Molly smiled at her friend's typical comment but she could not completely relax. She tried to recall the guests at the Fotherby party but was unable to remember if any of the other women had been tall, slim blondes. With a little sigh of resignation Molly decided that she would not actually die from embarrassment anyway. It was only one night and she would be spending most of the time in the kitchen. Whatever Mrs Roysten thought, if indeed she thought anything, it could just slide over Molly's head.

It was in this slightly belligerent frame of mind that Molly arrived at the Roysten house which was an imposing two-storeyed residence of white brick, set in grounds which had been extensively landscaped. Beth drove around to what had been pointed out to her as the tradesmen's entrance.

There was no need to announce their arrival and they immediately set about transferring all the food from the van to the kitchen. Here the work areas were more than adequate and no expense had been spared on every facility a demanding cook could require. Beth was checking over the dinner service and pointing out to Molly the uses of the silver serving-dishes when Mrs Roysten made her appearance.

With a gracious smile of welcome on her skilfully made-up face she swept into the kitchen and swept away Molly's last hope of a comfortable evening. There was no mistaking the woman and the smug satisfaction in her eyes told Molly that Mrs Roysten had not mistaken her identity either.

Molly's hackles rose, insisting that she had nothing to be ashamed of and if the woman made any reference to that scene with Richard Pembroke, then Molly would deliver a snub which would teach her to mind her own business. The matter was personal, private and closed.

'Good evening, Mrs Roysten,' Beth said in her best plummy voice. 'We have everything ready for you and I see you have everything ready for us. Thank you for remembering all our requirements. I'm sure you can look forward to a memorable dinner party.'

'Oh I'm sure it will be, Mrs Patterson. Very memorable,' she repeated with sly emphasis as she looked pointedly at Molly for an introduction.

Beth immediately obliged. 'This is my partner, Miss Fitzgerald. Mrs Roysten, Molly.'

'Molly ... What a quaint, old-fashioned name!'

The comment was altogether too saccharine for Molly's liking but she managed a polite smile. 'How do you do, Mrs Roysten.'

'I am so very pleased to have you two take the whole load off my shoulders. So nice to have a dinner party without having to worry about anything. Would you mind if I call you Molly and ... uh .. Beth, isn't it? Fitzgerald and Patterson are rather a mouthful.'

It was Beth's turn to speak with sickly sweetness. She hated such liberties being taken for granted but a paying customer had to be indulged. 'As you wish, Mrs Roysten.'

'Oh good! I hate tripping over names. One feels such a fool. Now is there anything else you need?'

'No, thank you. We're all organised,' Beth assured her.

'Well then, I'll leave you to it. Eight o'clock for hors d'oeuvres in the lounge.'

'We have your timetable here, Mrs Roysten,' Beth pointed out with an indulgence which was definitely suspect.

An ingratiating smile was flashed. 'Of course. Silly of me. You girls are real professionals, aren't you? Oh, and Molly, would you serve the hors d'oeuvres? My husband was really quite taken by you at the . . . the Fotherby's party.'

The hesitation was only slight but it was enough to make Molly's heart sink. The scene at the Opera House was obviously a crystal clear memory and one which titillated them.

Mrs Roysten pulled a wry grimace. 'He always has had an eye for redheads and your hair is such a distinctive shade.' Then as if to erase any possible offence taken she smiled again. 'I hope you don't object to being admired.'

'I'm not here to be admired, Mrs Roysten,' Molly said with a sharp edge of irony, 'but if it pleases you, I shall serve the hors d'oeuvres at eight o'clock.'

'Thank you. These men do have to be indulged occasionally,' she tossed off in mock exasperation as she made her exit from the kitchen.

Bitch! Molly seethed and had to take a good, hard hold on her temper. There had been a glint of malice in Mrs Roysten's baby-blue eyes on that last throwaway line. A horrible thought suddenly struck her. What if all the dinner guests had been at the ballet that night? What if Richard Pembroke was among them? Oh no! No one could be that mean and malicious, surely to God!

Her imagination was running to feverish lengths. No, this was surely just a private little joke between Mrs Roysten and her husband. Damn their eyes!

'I hate, hate, hate being patronised,' Beth grated as soon as the woman was safely out of earshot. 'Smooth, uppity, cat with the cream! We'll be earning our money tonight, Molly.'

'You can say that again,' Molly muttered grimly.

'Pity I've already given her our price.'

'What would you do? Triple it?'

Beth laughed. 'From the looks of their house they probably wouldn't even sneeze at that.' She sighed and gave a shrug of resignation. 'Oh well! As long as they're paying we dance to their tune.'

But the tune had some very sour overtones tonight, Molly thought to herself as she prepared the hors d'oeuvres tray, artistically arranging little pastry cases with creamed crab, neat rolls of smoked salmon, slices of chicken liver pâté on thin pieces of toast, savoury biscuits topped with creamed cheese and olives, pickled quails' eggs, diced ham and salami. Beth was busy with the oyster soup which was her speciality. They heard the front doorbell chime several times and the gradual build-up of conversation and laughter as more guests joined the company.

'Eight o'clock. Hang on to your hair,' Beth teased.

Molly picked up the tray and rolled her eyes. 'It's my tongue I'll have to hang on to, not my hair.'

'Grit your teeth and smile,' Beth advised as she held the door open.

Molly bared her teeth at her as she passed by into the dining room. An elegant archway led through to the lounge and she paused there for a moment to do a swift head-count, an automatic check that all the guests had arrived. The count was never completed. Richard Pembroke stood at the other end of the room.

Molly's heart stopped altogether. She froze. It was some moments before his wandering gaze caught her still figure in the archway. The sudden rigidity of his expression told her this meeting was a shock to him, too. They had both been set up. Anger re-ignited the pumping of her heart. Her eyes swept around the company, noting the amused little smiles as glances darted between the two antagonists. Conversation had died to a murmur.

So they had anticipated a scene! God damn their mean little hearts! No way was Molly going to give them what they wanted. She fixed a serene expression on her face and sailed down the room, determined to do her job as if the whole company were complete strangers. Which they were. And would remain so. Exacting the utmost control on her facial muscles Molly smiled at Mrs Roysten and offered the tray to her and her closest companions.

'Mmmm. It all looks so appetising,' one of them crooned. 'I don't know what to choose. What's in the little pastry cases?'

'Creamed crab,' Molly replied smoothly and was pleased to find her voice in normal working order.

She passed on to the next group, pricklingly aware of Richard Pembroke's presence, standing beside a seated woman and next to a man as tall as himself.

The tall man spoke. 'Thank you, Molly. I'm Ted Roysten and may I say how delighted we are to have you with us tonight.'

She lifted her lashes and looked him straight in the eye. 'I hope you'll be delighted with the menu we've prepared, Mr Roysten.'

'Oh, I have no doubts on that score,' he retorted, and the amusement in his eyes sickened Molly. 'The meal you gave us at the Fotherbys' was superb. In fact I don't think I've ever eaten better food.'

He was deliberately holding her there to feed off her reaction to the situation. Molly smiled. 'Thank you, Mr Roysten. Now, if you'll excuse me, I have to see to your guests' needs.'

'Miss Fitzgerald . . .'

It took all Molly's grit to keep her composure and respond politely to that voice. Everything within her bristled with antagonism, but somehow she managed a façade of calm innocence as she met the grey eyes which had cut her with contempt. The eyes did their best to pierce her façade but she determinedly kept it intact.

'. . . I see you do not wish to know me.' The soft comment held a wry note.

'I do not know you, sir,' Molly replied, then added sweetly, 'except as a guest at this dinner party. I hope you enjoy the evening.'

Before he could say another word she was off and offering the tray of hors d'oeuvres to another group. Molly did the rounds a couple more times and, much to her relief, Richard Pembroke made no further attempt to speak to her or draw her attention. When at last she could withdraw to the kitchen, Molly closed the door behind her with feeling and leaned against it for support. She suddenly felt very shaky.

'What's the matter?' Beth frowned at her. 'You've gone as white as a sheet, Molly.'

'I hate that woman and I hate that man and I don't know how I'm going to get through the rest of the evening.' Molly took a deep breath and pushed herself away from the door. 'But I'm not going to let them think they've got to me,' she added with stubborn pride.

Beth pulled a commiserating grimace. 'As bad as that, huh?'

'You don't know the half of it,' Molly said with ironic truth.

'I'll do the rest of the serving if you like,' Beth offered.

Molly considered it for a few moments then shook her head. Pride would not allow her to let it appear that she was avoiding Richard Pembroke. The Roystens had set up this little game but as the star performer Molly could play it any way she liked. Whatever words she spoke were her own and perhaps she could put a twist in their miserable tails.

'No. I've got their measure now,' she said with slow deliberation. 'In fact you can leave all the serving to me. I think I might even enjoy it, given a certain amount of black humour.'

'Molly, watch yourself,' Beth cautioned with a

concerned lowering of the eyebrows.

'Not to worry, Beth. I'll be all sweetness and light,' Molly promised, giving her a brilliantly false smile.

CHAPTER FOUR

THE guests were all seated. The first dinner wine had been poured. In the kitchen the thick, creamy soup had been ladled out. Beth and Molly worked quickly in tandem, first the avocado garnish, then the single fat oyster, topped by a dob of cream and a fine sprinkle of chives. Molly picked up the first tray-load, Beth opened the door for her and the first course was on its way.

Fortunately the three-metre maghogany dining-table allowed the ten people to sit comfortably around it and still gave Molly room to serve with ease. She did not have to lift dishes over shoulders. Unfortunately the spacious seating tended to spotlight her and she was very conscious of eyes following her every movement around the table. The pause in the conversation aggravated her self-consciousness. It was an effort to keep her hand steady as she lifted each soup plate off the tray and on to the table, and she walked with a very straight back on her return to the kitchen for the second tray-load.

Richard Pembroke sat to the right and one lady removed from his host. Molly decided to begin her second trip of serving with him before the watching eyes could rattle her composure. Nevertheless it was still an effort to keep her hand steady as she leaned past him, and only the

44

most disciplined will-power kept her from spilling the soup when he spoke.

'I apologise.'

It was barely a whisper in her ear, inaudible to anyone else. Molly managed to set the soup down safely. She squashed the impulse to reject his words. Any retort or pause near Richard Pembroke would be noted by the company and she was determined not to give their avaricious eyes food for speculative thought. She gripped the tray a little harder and continued her waitressing. It was not until she had passed around her hostess and on to the other side of the table that Ted Roysten fired his first shot.

'A hot dish, eh, Richard?' he drawled loudly.

It got to Molly. The double meaning was emphasised by the smirk on Ted Roysten's mouth as he looked pointedly at her and then to his guest. A hot flush crept over her skin and she darted a challenging glare at Richard Pembroke. Let him smile or say anything dubious and she would throw the whole damned tray at him.

His face was an inscrutable mask. He dropped his gaze to the plate before him. 'You're making an assumption, Ted. Assumptions can be wrong,' he stated quietly.

'Indeed!'

The gloating chuckle made Molly bristle.

'Well, I can hardly correct a QC. You barristers are past masters at making assumptions.'

He was rubbing it in with glee, thoroughly enjoying the discomfort he was creating. Molly's hostility switched direction and a burst of adrenalin made her hand rock-steady as she placed the last plate of soup in front of Ted Roysten.

'It is hot, sir, so do be careful,' she said sweetly. 'If you spilt it in your lap it could do you a nasty damage.'

She flashed a smile of totally transparent innocence down the length of the table, caught the appreciative twitch of Richard Pembroke's lips, and marched out of the dining room, head high, ignoring the titters behind her.

Molly seethed with fury as she helped Beth place the prepared pheasants in the oven. She imagined putting Richard Pembroke and the Roystens on a spit and slowly roasting them. Her sense of fairness forced a correction of that thought. Richard Pembroke could not be blamed for tonight's little torture.

And he had apologised. Not that a couple of soft words made up for his former scornful judgment of her. Still, he had indirectly conceded that he had made false assumptions. She supposed that was quite a concession from a man like Richard Pembroke. A QC? Molly's mouth curled. The profession suited him right down to the ground. He was just the type to hammer some poor, helpless wretch in the witness-box. His apology was annoying in that it made it difficult for her to keep nursing a grievance against him. She even felt a sneaking sympathy for him. He was in the hot-seat well and truly, while she at least had the kitchen as a refuge.

When it was time to collect the soup plates Molly girded herself mentally against the subtle attack which she knew would inevitably come. She was the bunny tonight and the Roystens would not give up their game because of one little counter-strike. She could only bare her teeth. They were going to make a meal of her.

'Best oyster soup I've ever tasted!' Ted Roysten boomed as soon as she re-entered the dining room.

'I'm glad you enjoyed it, sir,' Molly said, deftly removing the plates as quickly as possible.

'Wouldn't you like to have Molly cooking for you all the time, Richard?' Mrs Roysten remarked, a snide insinuation mixed in with her patronising tone.

Cooking! They obviously wanted to make her boil over. Molly took up the bait and defused it. 'The soup is my partner's speciality, Mrs Roysten. I had no hand in it.'

'Amanda, ask her for the recipe,' Ted Roysten instructed his wife.

'You must know it, Molly. You work in the kitchen alongside Beth,' she prompted silkily.

The remark somehow sounded as if Molly was no more than a scullery maid. 'Good cooks are artists, Mrs Roysten, and artists don't give away their trade secrets. If anyone at all could produce what we do, our talents wouldn't command such high fees,' she explained with her own little touch of condescension.

Molly felt quite pleased with her little speech. No offence could be taken from it but it asserted her worth and she approached Richard Pembroke without trepidation. It flashed through her mind that she should make some acknowledgment of his

apology but she did not wish to be seen speaking
to him and there seemed little point to starting up
a dialogue between them. They were hardly likely
to ever meet again. She reached for his plate,
aware that all eyes were upon them.

'There are not my friends.'

The low murmur startled her. She hesitated
fractionally then quickly recovered, going on to
retrieve the last few plates in a smooth flow
before making a dignified exit.

Not his friends! The words echoed around
Molly's mind as she kept a careful eye on the fish
she was steaming. Beth finished washing the soup
plates and started on the sauce for the entrée. For
the most part they worked in silence, concentrat-
ing on what they were doing for ultimate results.
They prided themselves on not making mistakes
with over-cooking or under-cooking. Molly,
however, was hopelessly distracted from her task
tonight.

Not his friends. What was Richard Pembroke
implying? That while he was with these people he
was not of them? Then what was he doing here
and why did he want to deny them to her? Why
should he care if she lumped him with them? But
he obviously did care or he would not have
bothered making such a point. It was almost as if
he cared about her opinion of him. Well, she had
given him that at the ballet in no uncertain terms.

But now he had apologised and admitted that
he had been wrong. Maybe he was not such a bad
person after all. And if she was completely fair,
he had probably been very upset at the ballet,
seeing his sister's husband with another woman.

Not that that exonerated him from saying what he had. But perhaps it was forgivable. In the circumstances. And he had apologised.

Molly sighed from the circling weight of her thoughts and tested the fish with a fork. It was tender. 'Sauce ready?' she asked Beth.

'Just a few more seconds. You can start.'

Molly carefully lifted the rolls of whiting on to the entrée plates. Beth followed with the sauce. Molly added sprigs of parsley. She picked up the first tray, took a deep breath and headed once more for the battle arena.

'This looks interesting. What exactly is it, Molly?' Amanda Roysten asked, apparently determined that Molly play the role of clever little cook.

Molly kept serving as she replied, intent on having the tray empty by the time she finished speaking. 'Fillets of whiting, Mrs Roysten, wrapped around a mixture of prawns and scallops and coated with hollandaise sauce.'

She didn't quite succeed.

'Sounds delectable, doesn't it, Richard?' Ted Roysten crowed. 'As delectable as the lady who's serving it.'

'I'd have to disagree with you, Ted,' came the smooth retort. 'The food may be delectable . . .' He paused then added softly, 'The lady is unique.'

Molly could not resist a sceptical look at Richard Pembroke and was surprised by the open admiration in his eyes. She flushed and swiftly withdrew for the second tray-load. The man was most confusing. First an apology and now admiration. She did not know what to make of him. Why should he admire her when she had so bitterly cut him in public? It had to be a pose to sabotage the Roysten game.

With her composure reconstructed Molly returned to the dining room to complete the serving of the entrée. She could not repress a little flutter of anticipation as she approached Richard Pembroke. Would he make another little aside? Unconsciously her head bent closer to his as she leaned past his shoulder.

'We were both set up,' he whispered.

'Richard . . .' Amanda Roysten called out.

Molly straightened with a jerk.

' . . . you know, seeing Molly next to you like that, I could swear I've seen you both together before tonight.'

With inward horror Molly thought the claws were about to be unsheathed. Richard Pembroke smoothly clipped them.

'I regret to say I've not had the pleasure of Miss Fitzgerald's company.'

'Pleasure?' Ted Roysten laughed. 'No. I daresay you haven't.'

It was too close to the bone for Molly's comfort. She put the last plate in front of Ted Roysten and escaped to the kitchen.

Set up! She had been set up through a business commitment. But she did not understand how Richard Pembroke had been inveigled into accepting this dinner invitation if the Roystens were not his friends. Nor did she understand why he stayed on at their table, taking what they were dishing out. Still, they hadn't got the better of him so far. And she was holding her own against their little snipes. Pride! That was it! Richard Pembroke was not a man to run away from an attack, any more than Molly would. He would face them down every inch of the way.

Her judgment of him was vindicated and the situation clarified when she went to remove the entrée plates.

'That dish was superb, Molly,' Amanda Roysten commented.

'Melted in the mouth,' one of the guests declared.

And another, 'Never had a more delicious entrée.'

'Would you like to get your own back?' Richard Pembroke murmured.

'What was that, Richard?' Ted Roysten instantly queried.

'I was thanking Miss Fitzgerald. The entrée would have delighted any gourmet.'

'Aha! There's an admission. You see, Molly, I had a bet with my friend here. That merely by picking up the telephone I could give him the best meal he's ever had. You'll have to capitulate before this night's over, Richard.'

'I never capitulate, Ted. I might concede but I never capitulate.'

Ted Roysten's smile was smug. 'Surely that's a legal nicety.'

'You think so?' was the very dry retort.

Molly carried away the impression that Ted Roysten had challenged a very formidable opponent. Richard Pembroke was no clay pigeon to be shot down without a fight. He might have been set up with a bet but he was contemplating turning the tables on the Roystens.

His suggestion loitered in Molly's mind as she automatically performed her chores; washing the entrée dishes, putting the dinner plates in the warmer, starting on the apple-brandy sauce for the pheasants. Beth was busy with the vegetables. They did not talk. Molly had plenty of time to think.

How to get her own back? She would like that. Very much indeed. But she couldn't see any way to embarrass those insensitive people out there. Or even make them squirm a little. All she could really do was avoid their verbal snares or snap back in a way they did not expect. She wondered if Richard Pembroke had a plan in mind. Curiosity and a relish for revenge prompted her decision. She would speak to him.

She took the sauce off the hotplate, removed the pheasants from the oven and carved them up while Beth arranged the cooked vegetables in the silver serving-dishes provided. When everything was ready they both worked quickly to transfer the main course to the dining-table, Beth taking the vegetables and the sauceboat while Molly put around the dinner plates with the meat.

Whether Beth's presence deterred pointed comment or the wine had mellowed their tongues, the Roystens did not draw attention to Molly this time. Conversation continued to flow around the table and Molly felt it was quite safe to say her few words to Richard Pembroke.

'I'd love to,' she muttered close to his ear and her eye caught the slight curve of his mouth. He had heard and her response had given him satisfaction.

Beth and she could relax while the main course was eaten. There was plenty of time to cook the dessert course. Molly made some instant coffee and they sat on the kitchen stools, glad to give their feet a rest.

'They asked for your oyster soup recipe,' she told Beth.

'Huh! Over my dead body.'

'Want me to recite the compliments?'

Beth gave a tired smile. 'I'll take them for granted. How are you coping with the upper class? Are they still getting under your skin?'

'Oh, I could cheerfully choke the lot,' Molly said lightly.

'Getting any flack from the handsome gent?'

Flack was Beth's term for the unwelcome attentions some male guests indulged in once they had a few drinks under the belt. Waitresses' bottoms seemed irresistible to them. Molly did not question whom Beth meant. Richard Pembroke was the only man at the dining-table who could be called handsome.

'No. None at all. What made you ask?'

Beth shrugged. 'He couldn't take his eyes off you as you served the pheasant. Very taken, I'd say. Watch out for the wandering hand.'

'He's been taken, all right. But not by me,' Molly muttered.

'What do you mean?'

It was Molly's turn to shrug. 'I get the impression he doesn't like the company any more than I do.'

'Well, I'm warning you. He fancies you.'

Molly frowned. Richard Pembroke fancying her? Impossible. How could a man fancy a woman who had tongue-lashed him in public? It just so happened that they were in the same boat tonight. He had merely been watching her for some reaction to his words. All the same, she was pricklingly aware of him when she returned to the dining room to clear away the main course. He turned his head towards her just as she reached for his plate and she almost backed away when his lips brushed her hair.

'I need your co-operation.'

Co-operation! With him? To do what? Molly had no time to think. As she went to pass by Ted Roysten her hand was caught and firmly held. This was no wandering hand which had hers captured, but a strongly purposeful one. A chill ran down Molly's spine. The game was about to restart.

'Ah, Molly, you must pause a moment and be my witness. After all, you're an interested party.'

The mocking cajolery increased the chill. Molly could not escape Ted Roysten's grasp without making a scene of it and the glint in his eyes told her he would relish that.

'If I'm an interested party, sir, then I'd be no good as a witness,' she pointed out in frustration.

He chuckled. 'Listen to her. Why, I do believe Molly would rival you at arguing a point, Richard.'

'I'd be proud to own Miss Fitzgerald as my equal.'

Molly could not help looking her surprise at

Richard Pembroke. The grey eyes assured her he spoke the truth and she felt oddly gratified that he did not consider himself superior to her.

'You're very generous with your admissions tonight,' Ted Roysten drawled. 'So let us now hear another one. Has this or has this not been the best meal you've ever had?'

Anticipation breathed from every face around the table. Molly tensed. She was on trial and the guests were expecting to get their vicarious thrills.

Richard Pembroke gave a dry chuckle, puncturing the tension with the relaxed sound of amusement. 'Really, Ted, you are a master of the embarrassing situation. You think by making me give my decision in front of Miss Fitzgerald, you could make me say that which is not true. You did not need to do that. The meal was magnificent. I may have had its equal. I've never had finer.'

'Nothing you want to criticise?'

Clearly Ted Roysten was disappointed with the answer, despite having won his bet. He had held Molly there for Richard Pembroke to publicly criticise her performance. He should have known by now that his taunting game was not producing the reactions he wanted.

'How can one criticise perfection?'

Molly felt even more gratified. She actually smiled at Richard Pembroke. He smiled back and suddenly he looked very handsome indeed.

'Hmmph,' grumbled his host. 'I didn't expect you to be won over so easily.'

'One so rarely meets true quality, Ted, that it

would be a mean man indeed who didn't
appreciate it.'

The other guests chorused their praise of the
meal, thus proving their lack of meanness.
Richard Pembroke's smile grew broader. Molly's
hand was abruptly released. She returned to the
kitchen with a pleasant little glow in her heart.
Richard Pembroke was really quite a nice person.
She wondered what kind of co-operation he
meant. Molly did not want to be involved in a
scene which might have repercussions on the
goodwill of the business. Harbouring vengeful
thoughts was one thing. Carrying them out was
a self-indulgence she couldn't afford. The
reputation of Dial-A-Dinner-Party had to be
safeguarded.

'We've just had our dinner declared perfection,'
she informed Beth. 'No finer food has ever been
served,' she added pompously.

Beth laughed with pleasure. 'Should've got
that on tape to use as an advertisement.' She was
arranging the cheese board with tiny bunches of
different-coloured grapes as a garnish. 'Here,
whizz this in while they're still patting their
stomachs and our backs.'

Molly placed the cheese board in front of the
hostess. Again her hand was caught, this time by
Amanda Roysten who looked up at her with
provocatively knowing eyes.

'You must be delighted to have won over such
a man as Richard, Molly. Some do consider him
God-almighty . . . on matters of food.'

The echo of her own taunt brought burning
spots of colour to her cheeks but Molly kept her

head. 'Then his judgment has even more value to us, Mrs Roysten.' She shot Richard Pembroke a warning look. 'This is our livelihood and our best advertisement is word-of-mouth.'

'Did you expect such an accolade from him?' the woman persisted.

'We pride ourselves on serving the finest food of its kind, Mrs Roysten.' And pride made Molly add, 'I was trained in Paris and Beth . . .'

'Paris! Really? I remember going to the ballet in Paris. *Giselle*, wasn't it, Ted?'

'I believe so, Amanda,' he chimed in. 'Though I must say I preferred *The Lyre Bird*. What did you think of it, Molly?'

'I didn't see *Giselle* in Paris,' she whipped back and snatched her hands from Amanda Roysten's grip. 'Please excuse me, Mrs Roysten. The dessert is my speciality and my performance in the kitchen is what you're paying me for.'

She could not help the bite in her voice and only barely restrained herself from slamming the kitchen door. She set about peeling the pears with a vicious swing of the knife. Oooh! How she'd love to get her own back on that bitch! She hoped that Richard Pembroke did have some viable scheme in mind. She would co-operate all right. She put the pears in a pan to steam and did quite a lot of steaming herself before melting into a wry smile.

It was ironic that she should be considering Richard Pembroke as a partner. Before tonight she would have contemptuously dismissed any such possibility. But then his attitude to her had undergone a vast change. Certainly he no longer considered her a scarlet woman and tonight he had virtually been her champion against the Roystens.

Molly lifted the pears out. Beth poured the strawberry purée over them and added the green slices of kiwi fruit while Molly placed perfect scoops of home-made ice-cream on each plate. With its contrast of colours the dessert was a very attractive one and drew appreciative comments from the guests as it was served.

Molly was tense, half-expecting a frontal assault from the Roystens now that they had advanced as far as the ballet. This was almost their last opportunity to get at her since there was only the coffee left to be served.

'Trust me,' Richard Pembroke said with quiet intensity as she placed the sweet in front of him.

'Yes,' she hissed in reply.

There was no move from Ted or Amanda Roysten to detain her. Molly withdrew, grimly sure that the Roystens were saving the finale of their party game for her last appearance. She hoped Richard Pembroke had something up his sleeve which would spike their guns. Blow the whole set-up back in their faces. With a bang.

As had been arranged, the Roystens directed their guests back into the lounge where the coffee was to be served. Their withdrawal from the dining room enabled Beth and Molly to clear the table quickly and complete the washing-up. They had done this and Molly was arranging a selection of after-dinner mints, rum balls and *petit fours* on a silver platter when Ted Roysten came into the kitchen, patting his stomach in expansive good humour.

'Ah, ladies! Splendid meal! Splendid service!' He produced a roll of notes.

Beth immediately came to the fore. 'I'm glad you were satisfied, Mr Roysten.' She checked the amount he had given her and smiled. 'I see you were very satisfied. Thank you.'

He laughed. 'Well, I won a little bet I had, and I must say, you ladies have been very accommodating.'

'Very,' Molly agreed sweetly.

Beth shot her a frown.

'Then we can count on you to bring in the coffee, Molly,' Ted Roysten slid out with oily charm.

'Oh, yes sir. You can count on it,' she replied with a dazzling smile which nonplussed him for a moment.

He looked sharply at her, frowned, then fixed another smile on his face. 'Well, thank you both for giving us such an enjoyable and relaxing evening. My wife particularly appreciated your services.'

'Laying it on a bit thick, weren't you, Molly?' Beth remarked as soon as he was gone.

'Whatever he paid us was blood money, and I'm telling you, Beth, we're not ever going to do another party for the Roystens or for anyone who gives them as a reference. They're poison.' She put the nibbles platter on to the trolley with the coffee service and nodded towards the door. 'This is the last act and I just hope Ted Roysten and his dear wife choke on it.'

Beth obliged with the door, her eyebrows upraised at the vehemence of Molly's feelings. 'Well, try to keep smiling,' she advised.

Molly's heart began thumping heavily on the long walk up the lounge. Amanda Roysten had a sly little smirk on her face. Molly's eyes darted hopefully towards Richard Pembroke. He had taken up a casual pose near the fireplace, one elbow resting on the mantel, a tiny glass of liqueur or port in his hand. He gave Molly a slight nod, so slight that she was not sure it was meant. She steered the trolly to Amanda Roysten's side. She felt every eye on her and every nerve in her body bristled with defence.

'Thank you, dear. Now before you go you must settle something for us . . .' The baby-blue eyes were gloating in anticipation of the kill.

'As your guest, Amanda, I claim the courtesy of being allowed to settle something first,' Richard Pembroke interrupted with smooth authority.

Ted Roysten laughed. 'Only too pleased to give you the opportunity, old boy.'

Richard Pembroke lifted one sardonic eyebrow at him then fixed his gaze on Molly. The grey eyes were not cold at all.

'I beg your indulgence for a few moments, Miss Fitzgerald. First let me congratulate you on a very fine meal. I would also like to express my admiration for the gracious manner in which it was served, under circumstances which would have been intolerable to a woman of less character and dignity. I apologise very sincerely for any strain placed on you by my presence here tonight.'

If he had been delivering a summary to a jury he could not have modulated his voice to greater effect. The pauses, the changes in tone, the subtle emphasis he gave the words; all proclaimed a master of rhetoric. Everyone was mesmerised into silence and he continued uninterrupted.

'I was grievously at fault in manner and speech when I spoke to you at the ballet some weeks ago. My host and my hostess and my fellow-guests tonight all heard your reply to me, a reply which they may not have realised was richly deserved. It is a very chastening thing to be found at fault on the very things I have always prided myself on. You did humble my pride, Miss Fitzgerald, and rightly so. A woman of honour could not have done less.

'While this party tonight may have been conceived with some ... shall we say, a little embarrassing amusement in mind ...' The cold stare he gave the Roystens froze the curls of their mouths into grimaces, but his expression softened again as he returned his gaze to Molly. '... I'd like to point out that Miss Fitzgerald has no cause for embarrassment. Her forthright defence of herself was justified. And I have no cause for embarrassment. Shame, yes, but not embarrassment. I had unjustly cast a slur on Miss Fitzgerald's character which I later found to be beyond reproach. I am grateful to have this opportunity to plead forgiveness for the wrong I did her.'

He lifted the pitch of his voice and it suddenly took on the sharp, condemnatory tone Molly remembered so well. 'I am also ashamed to have

accepted hospitality from people who find
enjoyment in humiliation of any kind, and now
that my conscience is considerably lighter, I shall
take my leave of you with the wish that our
acquaintance shall never be renewed.'

Any trace of smiles had long been wiped from
faces. The general expression of the whole party
was one of stunned affront, completely ignored
by Richard Pembroke as he strode over to Molly
and took her hand. His eyes held a wry gleam as
he spoke softly to her.

'Miss Fitzgerald, I hope, should we ever meet
again, you will do me the honour of recognising
me.'

Molly was a little thunderstruck herself from
his eloquence on her behalf. She found her
tongue with difficulty. 'I believe I would
recognise the gentleman you've been tonight, Mr
Pembroke.'

'I wanted to redeem myself in your eyes, Miss
Fitzgerald. I hope I have. Can you leave now?' he
asked in some concern.

'Yes. Thank you.'

He smiled. 'Then I wish you good night.'

Her responding smile granted him more than
forgiveness. 'Good night, Mr Pembroke.'

They both turned away, he towards the front
door, she towards the kitchen, leaving a dumb-
struck group behind them with considerable
satisfaction. Honour had been avenged once
again.

CHAPTER FIVE

'LETTER for you.'

Beth tossed it on the bench where Molly was dicing the meat for the lamb navarin which had been ordered for tonight.

'Not Mum's writing,' she commented, frowning in puzzlement over the boldly penned address. Each letter had been stroked with precision, a sharp contrast to her mother's rounded style.

Molly received and replied to a weekly letter from her mother who remained determinedly settled in Taree, a mid-north coast town where she had lived all her life; born, married and widowed there, and fully intending to die there. She visited Sydney three or four times a year to see Molly and do some shopping but she couldn't abide the hustle and bustle of city life for long.

Connor, Molly's brother, was in Canada but he only ever wrote to his mother, who passed any news on to Molly. Besides, the handwriting on the envelope was not Connor's either and the letter had not been posted airmail. Unable to repress her curiosity any longer, Molly scooped the meat into a bag for its coating of flour and quickly washed her hands.

The envelope was of good, thick paper, undoubtedly taken from quality stationery. She slit it open and extracted a folded piece of notepaper. Something fluttered to the floor. It looked like a ticket of some kind. Molly picked it up and was astonished to find it was indeed a ticket, and for a ballet performance of *Anna Karenina* in four days' time.

Her heart leapt in excitement. She had been tempted to buy a ticket when bookings had become available but the memory of her last attendance at a ballet had soured the temptation. But actually having a ticket in hand ... her reluctance to go disappeared as if it had never been.

But who had sent it to her? She swiftly unfolded the notepaper and her eyes skimmed the short message.

Dear Miss Fitzgerald,

As a woman of honour you will understand that a man of honour cannot rest easily until all his debts are discharged. I would like you to enjoy this ballet since I ruined the last one for you. Please accept this token of my regret and consider it no more than just compensation.

Yours sincerely,
Richard Pembroke

The curve of Molly's mouth grew slowly wider as she read until she had to laugh. Richard Pembroke was not a man to do anything by halves. Oh no! Give him his due. When he set his mind on doing something he went all the way.

'What's so funny?' Beth asked curiously.

Unable to stop gurgling with amusement Molly shook her head and handed Beth the note

and the ticket. Beth had overheard Richard
Pembroke's pointed speech at the Roystens'. She
had felt appehensive about Molly's attitude over
the serving of the coffee and had hovered near the
archway, ready to jump in and smooth over any
upset. She had found the speech quite mind-
boggling and Molly had been pressured into
explaining the whole background to it on the way
home. Strangely enough it had not hurt her to
speak of Jeremy's deception, or that wretched
scene at the ballet. Somehow those wounds had
been cauterised by Richard Pembroke's acceptance and vindication of her behaviour.

Beth was not amused by the letter. She
frowned over it. 'You want to watch him. He's
after something. No one gives anything away
without a purpose,' she declared suspiciously.

'Oh, Beth! What could he be after?' Molly
mocked.

Beth gave her a funny look. 'Maybe he's after
you. I thought he fancied you at the Roystens'
party.'

Molly grimaced with exasperation. 'I told you
all about that. He only wanted an answer from
me.'

'And all those things he said,' Beth continued,
undeterred by Molly's protest. 'It sounded to me
as if he wanted to win you over. Make you see
him as a knight in shining armour.'

'Oh, Lordy!' Molly sighed. 'Just listen to
yourself. Finding worms in every can. It's not
like that, Beth.'

'A ticket to the ballet isn't peanuts,' Beth
argued.

'It probably is to a QC. Anyhow, as he said in his letter, he owes me that.'

'Men! You just can't trust them,' came the conclusive grumble.

'I don't know about that. I trusted Richard Pembroke at the Roystens' and he sure turned up trumps,' Molly grinned. 'Anyhow, I'm going to use the ticket and go to the ballet. We've only got deliveries that night so there's no problem.'

Gina came bustling in with the ingredients for the Italian dishes she was to cook for their bookings and the conversation turned to the work ahead of them. Only briefly did Molly's mind linger on Beth's suspicions. They were ridiculous. Far-fetched. There was simply no basis for thinking that Richard Pembroke was interested in her as a woman.

A woman of honour. The phrase flitted through her thoughts. She liked it. A man of honour. That was precisely the kind of man Molly wanted. Someone she could trust to always stand by her, to love and honour from this day forth ... She shook off the whimsical train of thought and got on with browning the meat in the frying pan. Day-dreaming about marriage was hardly a profitable exercise, particularly when there was no substance behind it.

The *Anna Karenina* ballet was not being performed at the Opera House but at the Regent Theatre. Molly was running late and she fought a sense of panic as she drove up floor after floor of the nearby multi-storey car park, with not a space in sight. Not until she reached the top floor was she able to park her small Datsun. Despairing of getting to the theatre on time she ran for the lift, tapped her foot impatiently as it made its sluggish way down, then ran again, punishing the thin heels of her elegant sandals. The lights were dimming and the orchestra already playing as she was ushered down the aisle to her seat. She sank into it with a sigh of relief, pleased that she hadn't missed anything.

'I'm glad you made it.'

The quiet voice drew her startled attention. 'You!' she squeaked in disbelief.

The grey eyes crinkled as Richard Pembroke smiled his pleasure. 'I'm glad, too, that you recognise me.'

Molly almost swallowed her tongue. She looked blankly at the curtained stage, took a few gulping breaths which helped to clear her throat, then looked again at Richard Pembroke. He was still smiling at her.

'What are you doing here?' she demanded abruptly.

'I like ballet. I rarely miss a show.' He lifted one hand in mute appeal. 'Do you object to my sitting next to you?'

How could she object when she was using the ticket he had sent her? And did she want to object? Her eyes questioned his uncertainly.

He suddenly grinned. 'I promise not to eat potato chips or crunchy lollies.'

She could not help smiling at the idea of him doing anything so juvenile. 'In that case, I don't mind if you stay.'

'Thank you.'

The music built to a crescendo and the curtains parted. Molly's attention automatically turned to the stage. It was some moments before she realised that her mind had not registered any part of the dance and her heart was not beating at all regularly. Shock, she told herself, and sternly commanded her faulty part to perform in a normal manner. She concentrated on ignoring the fact that Richard Pembroke occupied the seat beside her. She had come to see the ballet and see it she would.

Unfortunately the dances of the first half of the programme comprised the more modern concepts in ballet and did not carry a story. While technically brilliant and brilliantly performed, they did not evoke the emotional involvement which could captivate Molly's whole attention. Her mind kept wandering to the man next to her.

Could Beth be right? Was Richard Pembroke interested in pursuing a relationship with her? What else could he mean by arranging this situation? The ticket had been enough to clean the slate between them. He was such a confusing, unpredictable man, she did not know what to make of him. She turned her head to look at him again, a frown of puzzlement creased between her eyes.

He caught her scrutiny and raised a quizzical eyebrow. Molly immediately returned her gaze to the stage, privately blessing the darkness which hid the rush of blood to her cheeks. She felt his eyes on her and cursed her awareness of him. What was she going to do if he did show a personal interest? Did she want to let Richard

Pembroke into her life? The question teased her mind continually and she had still not found an answer to it when the curtain closed and the lights came up for the interval. In hopeless indecision Molly sat on in her seat, studiously ignoring the man next to her yet intensely aware that he had not moved either.

'Would you accompany me out for a glass of champagne? I believe I owe you that, too.'

The tone of his voice was soft, deep, pleasant. Molly blushed to the roots of her hair, recalling all too vividly the toast Jeremy had made just as Richard Pembroke had come on the scene all those weeks ago. She vaguely remembered thrusting the glass back at Jeremy before accosting her erstwhile judge. She plucked at the blue silk of her second-best dress in an agony of embarrassment until a spark of pride gave her the courage to face him.

'Mr Pembroke, thank you for sending me the ticket. It was kind and thoughtful of you. I like ballet very much, so I came. I didn't expect you to be here. I don't know why you should plan that I sit next to you. You could have bought any other seat in the theatre.'

The slight smile held a touch of whimsy, and to her further confusion the grey eyes were very warm. 'I preferred ... hoped ... to have the pleasure of your company, Miss Fitzgerald.'

She swallowed hard. It was true then. He was interested in her. And now the ball was in her court. She had to decide. 'Are you married, Mr Pembroke?' she burst out bluntly.

His slight frown held a pained understanding.

'No, I'm not married, Miss Fitzgerald,' he assured her solemnly.

Molly's cheeks burnt brightly but she stubbornly persisted. 'Have you a relationship with anyone who would object to seeing me in your company?'

His gaze met her direct blaze without the tiniest waver. 'I've given no one any personal claim on me, nor am I committed to any person in the sense you mean. Should anyone suggest such an objection exists, Miss Fitzgerald, be assured that I will set them straight in the clearest possible terms.' His mouth curved slightly. 'I'm not known to be short of words when I wish to express myself.'

Her smile was almost a grin, her blue eyes dancing their appreciation of his performance at the Roystens'. 'I'll grant you that, Mr Pembroke. I doubt anyone could match you.'

'Oh, I believe you could, Miss Fitzgerald,' he drawled, his eyes dancing their reminder of her performance.

She laughed. The past had been put in its proper perspective. Mistakes corrected. 'I shall accept your offer of champagne, Mr Pembroke, if for no other reason than to affirm that you owe me nothing more.'

He rose to his feet and Molly was instantly reminded of how impressive a figure he was. She felt a little overwhelmed by him as he tucked her arm into his and led her out to the foyer bar. Although he found her a vacant chair she declined to sit down, preferring to stretch her legs and feeling an instinctive need to stand up to Richard Pembroke, asserting an equality she was not at all sure existed.

She watched him go to the bar. Other people automatically made room for him. He was quickly served. There was an aura of authority about him which would always command quick service. It had been Molly's first impression of him and now she saw it confirmed. Looked at objectively he was not really handsome, but he had an indefinable presence which drew eyes to him. A distinctive man. A very attractive man. A man who could stamp himself indelibly on anyone's memory.

The thought drifted into Molly's mind and caught. It seemed incredible yet she found it difficult now to recall Philippe's features exactly. His face was a haze, overlaid by painful memories. Her memory conjured up Jeremy's face with no trouble at all, but she saw it in her mind's eye as lacking the strength and character which belonged to Richard Pembroke. The easy charm and devil-may-care personality which had so characterised Jeremy had been much of his attraction, but they had been shallow attributes. She had been a fool to have fallen under his spell. A gullible fool. Just as she had been with Philippe.

'Why the frown?'

She met the grey eyes and saw concern. It gave her a nice, warm feeling to have this man concerned on her behalf. He seemed so well equipped to handle and beat any problem. 'Oh, I was just reviewing my life,' she said with a touch of wry sadness. 'It's not remarkable for its moments of great wisdom.'

He handed her a glass and clicked it with his. 'To a new beginning,' he said softly.

She smiled. 'Is that ever possible?'

'I'd like to think so,' he replied seriously. 'I hope you and I can do that tonight. Is it possible?'

Her heart started pumping at a crazy rate. Molly sipped her champagne in an effort to calm herself. He was serious. He was seriously interested in her. And yes, she wanted him to be. Despite the wine her mouth felt very dry.

'Yes. I'd like that,' she finally got out, more emphatically than she had planned on.

He smiled and there was no hint of triumph in his eyes, no suggestion that he exulted in having manipulated a surrender from her. They sparkled with pure, unadulterated happiness. 'Is Molly your christened name?'

'No. It's Melissa. But everyone's always called me Molly.'

'May I?'

'Please do.'

'I'd be pleased if you'd call me Richard.'

'Then I shall.'

He lifted his glass. 'Let's drink to that.'

And they did. Molly's head felt quite dizzy.

'What did you think of the first half of the programme?' he asked interestedly.

'The choreography was a bit too modern for my taste,' she replied truthfully. 'I can admire the dancers' grace and technical brilliance but I prefer something with more soul. I like the story ballets best.'

'So do I. You'll like *Anna Karenina*.'

'Have you seen it before?'

He shook his head. 'I've read the book. The story is one of strong passions. Very Russian.'

'The only Russian novel I've read is *War and Peace*.'

'I hope that's a good omen for us. The "peace" part anyway.'

She lifted her glass to him in a teasing salute. 'Well, you've certainly done your part in making it acceptable.'

'The effort was rewarding.' He smiled and this time the smile was rich with satisfaction.

It curled Molly's stomach.

'Do you like reading?' he asked.

'I'm a terrible book-worm. I'll devour anything,' she replied quickly, relieved that he had turned the conversation on to less personal ground.

He did not leave it there. 'I had a feeling we'd have much in common.'

'But you hardly know me,' she protested weakly. He was leaping ahead, going too far too fast, and she didn't want that, ever again.

'What I do know, I like very much. And I'd like to know more. Much more,' he stated with a quiet intensity of purpose which Molly found even more disturbing.

Intuition whispered that this was a man who could reach inside her, know her in a way no other person had even approached, and the very thought of such power frightened her, because she would no longer belong to herself, the self she relied upon to keep surviving no matter what happened.

She gulped down the rest of her champagne just as the warning bell rang to signal patrons back to their seats. Richard disposed of the empty glass for her and again took her arm to walk her back into the theatre. She was glad of it. She felt quite shaky. It was a relief to sink into her seat and even more of a relief when the lights dimmed and she could get a hold on herself in the privacy of darkness.

The ballet began. Molly decided that it was stupidly premature to get herself fussed over Richard Pembroke's attentions. She was just having an unfortunate reaction, the result of making an adjustment from hostility to ... to something else. The magnificent costuming of the dancers gradually caught her gaze and held it. The clothes were beautiful, so very rich and so very Russian.

In a kind of belligerent self-defence Molly fastened her attention on the stage and was quickly swept up into the story being so poignantly portrayed by the dance; the determined pursuit of the married Anna by the dashing young Count Vronksy.

In no time at all Molly was identifying with Anna's emotions, living them with her; the initial response to flattery growing into fascination, and from there to passionate love, the terrible tug-of-war in Anna's heart ... the need to be with her lover fighting her love for her son and the loyalty due to her husband, then the fateful choice to give up everything for love of Count Vronsky, a love which was doomed by the betrayal of her sense of honour and the rigid society whose laws she had flouted.

The inevitable disintegration of the relationship under the dual strain of emotional and social pressures rent Molly's heart. She felt every nuance of Anna's growing despair, the agony of a love which slowly became more and more destructive, the insidious growth of jealousy and possessiveness as Anna was reduced to total dependency on Count Vronsky by a world which accepted him but rejected her. She had sacrificed everything for an illicit love and she was condemned for it.

The train which had provided the setting for Anna's first meeting with Count Vronsky, and which had symbolised the journeys of Anna's emotions, had to be the vehicle to bring the story to an end. It roared on to the stage, big, black, ominous. The sadness of Anna's last dance brought tears to Molly's eyes. They streamed unashamedly down her cheeks as the relentless, unfeeling wheels of the train churned on, unaware of the frail piece of humanity they were crushing, uncaring that a soul had given up in despair.

Molly felt the pain for Anna. The curtain closed. The lights came on. The audience clapped. Molly could not stop crying. She fumbled in her handbag for tissues. Richard passed her a handkerchief. She took it gratefully and tried to mop up the tears. Her heart ached so much there was no stopping them. The show was over. People were standing, moving out into the aisles. Molly could not move, not until she had brought herself under control.

She darted an apologetic look at Richard who

was calmly waiting beside her. 'I'm sorry. You must think me an awful fool.'

'Not at all. I think you're a woman of very deep feeling and compassion. Take your time, Molly. I'm in no rush,' he answered softly.

She took a deep breath. 'You ... you don't have to stay with me.'

'I want to stay with you.'

'I ... I don't want you to be embarrassed.'

'I'm not easily embarrassed.'

The dry intonation drew a watery smile from her. 'It's just that the ... the story ... was a bit close to me. He shouldn't have done it. It hurt her so much.'

'He wanted her.'

'But he must have known the consequences for her. It was so unfair.'

'Perhaps he wanted her so much he didn't want to see the consequences.'

She shook her head. 'He knew ... he knew ...'

'So did she, Molly.'

She took another deep breath and blinked back the last of the tears. 'Yes. You're right. But he made it very hard for her.'

'You would have turned him away.'

The flat certainty in his voice surprised her. She looked into eyes which held no shadow of doubt. The memory of her very public rejection of Jeremy flashed into her mind. Richard would most probably have heard the slap, if not the words.

'Yes, I would have,' she admitted wryly. 'I believe one should stick to a commitment as serious as marriage, especially when there are children. It's probably an old-fashioned belief but . . .'

'No, it's not old-fashioned. Promises should never be given unless the people involved are prepared to keep and honour them. Broken promises bring a lot of grief.' He sighed and added, 'I see a lot of the consequences in my profession.'

The law. Of course, he would, Molly realised. 'Do you like being a barrister?'

He smiled. 'Yes, I do. There's always a challenge to be met.'

'And won?'

His smile turned into a grin. 'Hopefully. Ready to go now?'

The theatre was empty, save for a group of ushers who were looking questioningly at them. Molly stood up, quelling a reluctance to leave. She would have liked to keep on talking to Richard. With a little sigh of disappointment she took the arm he offered her. They walked out to the street in a companionable silence.

'Did you come by car?' Richard asked.

'Yes. It's just down here in the car park.' She nodded in the direction and braced herself to take her leave of him. 'At the end of this block. No trouble at all. Thank you for . . . for being so kind to me,' she added shyly, unable to meet his eyes lest he perceive her wish to remain in his company.

'Must you go? I'd like you to have supper with me.'

Her lashes flew up in eagerness. 'I'd like that, too.'

He really had a lovely smile. 'Do you enjoy Chinese food?'

'Yes.' She didn't care what she ate. She didn't feel like food at all. But so long as she could be with him a little while longer, food was of no consequence.

The smile took on an ironic twist. 'I feel it's the greatest temerity to offer a cook of your calibre any kind of food, but I can trust Lee Kwong Wu to serve us the best. He also owns a small car park opposite his restaurant so if you'd like to drive your car there, it would save your worrying about it later.'

'All right,' she readily agreed. 'But you'll have to show me where to go.'

'I'll come with you. My car's already there. It's only a few streets away.'

She suddenly felt buoyant with happiness. 'Let's go then.'

The night was not over, she sang to herself. Why, it was really only beginning. Richard's words came back to her. A new beginning. Yes. That was how he made her feel. As if nothing in the past mattered any more. Somehow this moment was more intensely real to her than anything that had gone before. She glanced up at him, slightly awe-struck that everything could be so different. This man who had been her enemy . . . no, not an enemy . . . a man who had judged harshly because he believed in the same things she believed in . . . a man of honour who had handsomely redressed his wrongs . . . a man of honour.

CHAPTER SIX

MOLLY had driven around and through Chinatown hundreds of times on her trips to the markets. By day the area looked seedy and by night rather tawdry, with its red and gold lights and dark alleys. She would never have ventured into one of its restaurants without a man at her side, yet the room Richard led her into was far from tawdry.

It was like stepping into a fairy-tale Far East, rich with colour, exquisitely decorated with beautiful lamps, figurines and ornaments, and furnished with lavish luxury; a deep pile carpet under their feet, carved tables and chairs of darkly polished wood, and fantastic screens of glowing beauty set around some tables to give guests a sense of privacy.

A Chinese gentleman of indeterminate age and immaculately attired in a dinner-suit came beaming forward the moment they entered. 'Mr Pembroke, I am so delighted that you honour me and my house tonight, and with your lovely guest, too.'

'Good to see you, Lee,' Richard nodded.

The man bowed and bowed again in an excess of pleasure. 'I have the best table reserved for you. The chef is at your service. Please come. I will see that you have everything you wish.'

'Very kind of you,' Richard murmured as they were ushered to a corner table.

'Ah, Mr Pembroke, I can never repay you enough. My house is yours. Let me arrange for you something special. But first some wine?'

'Yes. Thank you.'

He snapped his fingers at a waiter, saw Molly and Richard comfortably seated, set up a magnificently embroidered screen, and when the waiter arrived with the wine, Lee took it from him, uncorked it and made a small ceremony of filling their glasses.

'Please enjoy. I will go and see to the food.'

Molly raised her eyebrows at Richard, curious and slightly overwhelmed by the VIP service. 'Do you come here often?'

To her surprise his grin had a sheepish look. 'No. Not often enough to Lee's mind. I got him off on a murder charge.'

'Murder!' Molly gasped in horror.

Richard shrugged. 'It wasn't really murder. I had the charge dropped to manslaughter which I then defended successfully. Lee considers he owes his freedom to me, but in my opinion he should never have been charged in the first place.'

Molly frowned in bewilderment. 'But he did kill someone?'

'Oh yes. Quite deliberately, too. At the time there was a vicious gang of thieves operating in Chinatown. The Chinese run family businesses and the gang had threatened families with knives to force their victims to tell where money was hidden on the premises. One woman had suffered multiple stab wounds. When the gang hit this restaurant, one of them held a knife to Lee's wife. Lee shot him.'

'Then it was self-defence.'

'Not technically. Lee himself wasn't being threatened. But he was driven by fear for his wife. In the same circumstances I would've shot the thug without compunction. A man should protect his woman from harm. I simply pointed that out to the jury.'

'Simply?' she queried with a sceptical look.

He chuckled. 'Well, perhaps with some emotional vehemence. If one isn't entitled to protect hearth and home, the law's a fool.'

'And you would protect hearth and home,' she said, testing out the depth of his convictions.

'With my life,' he answered firmly, and Molly could not doubt that he meant it.

A woman would feel safe with him, she decided. He would give his wife and family all the security he could. 'Why aren't you married?' she blurted out and then flushed at the blunt directness of the question. She tried to soften it. 'I mean, most men of your age are, and it's not as if . . . well, you're not unattractive.'

His eyes crinkled with amusement. 'Thank you, but at thirty-six I don't consider myself so very old. Do you?'

'No . . . no . . .' Her flush grew deeper. 'I guess thirty-six is about a man's prime,' she rushed out defensively.

He laughed. 'Well, I do hope so. I'd hate to think I was past it.' His eyes were teasing her, telling her he wasn't the least bit offended.

'You haven't answered my question,' she pointed out, wanting to know the answer. It was important to her, just as this man could be important to her, if she let him close. Already she had gone thus far in her acceptance of him and she did not want to leave it too late to turn back. Twice men had brought her grief. She did not want to invite it on herself again.

Richard instantly sobered as if he sensed the doubt in her mind. 'I've nothing against marriage. I envy those who are happily married.' His eyes held a soft irony. 'But it's not so easy to find someone with whom you actually want to live on a permanent basis.'

He shrugged. 'I was engaged to be married once. Perhaps it might have worked out, given the chance.' His mouth curled into a self-mocking smile. 'But I was a young man then with a young man's ego, and the woman I'd chosen refused to fit into the slot I insisted she inhabit as my wife. So I lost her.'

'What did you expect of her?' Molly asked curiously.

'Too much,' he admitted frankly. 'I was unreasonable. She was in law, too. We were both very keen to make names for ourselves. It annoyed me whenever she put her job ahead of any arrangement we'd made to see each other. She was very forthright, like you.'

He smiled and Molly understood that her forthrightness had actually attracted him.

'Anyway, she pointed out that I did exactly the same thing. And I did. I argued that since I was going to be the provider, my work was more important than hers. She replied that if that was my attitude, she was not going to marry a male chauvinist pig. My pride and her pride cemented the break.' He sighed and his eyes held a hard-learnt wisdom. 'The years have taught me that pride is a very cold bed-fellow. I don't intend that it ever get in the way again.'

He had certainly set it aside as far as she was concerned, Molly thought with some gratification. She wondered how deeply he regretted his broken engagement. 'Do you still love her?' she asked softly.

He looked surprised by the question. 'No. I don't think I knew what love was then. She was ... a challenge. Very beautiful, very bright, and about as self-centred as I was. I wanted to own her. But I'm glad now we didn't marry. And that isn't pride talking,' he added with dry humour.

She sighed with contentment. 'Well, I'm glad you didn't marry her, too. There aren't so many unattached males around for a girl of twenty-six, and there are too many attached ones who conveniently ignore their ties.'

His face became tight and closed and Molly instantly regretted the looseness of her tongue. She had momentarily forgotten that Jeremy was married to Richard's sister. It could only pain him to be reminded that a marriage so closely related to him had to be floundering for such infidelity to be contemplated, let alone carried as far as Jeremy had gone.

Molly could have sworn that Jeremy's avowals of love had been sincere. But maybe they had merely been the practised spiel of a habitual philanderer. His lovemaking had certainly been practised. He had aroused her with a finesse which had made his promises well-nigh irresist-ible to a girl who had been starved of love.

She shivered over the closeness of her surrender. It would have been a terrible mistake, a shameful mistake since she now knew that she had not loved him. She had been strongly attracted to him physically, lured into vulnerability by the romance of their meeting and the intoxication of being loved . . . or so she thought.

Molly was unaware of how bleak her own expression had become. The weariness of disillusionment whitened and dragged at her skin, The bright blue eyes had dulled to lifelessness. The corners of her mouth drooped.

'I'm sorry. I truly am sorry that Jeremy hurt you like that. I could wring his irresponsible neck.'

Her lashes fluttered up in surprise at the taut vehemence in Richard's voice. The compassion and anger was for her sake, not his sister's. Which did not seem right. She frowned. 'I'm sorry for your sister. I hope she never knows.'

'She won't if Jeremy has any sense at all,' he said bitingly, then shrugged off his moroseness and gave an ironic smile. 'That was not a good choice of ballet, was it? I'll do better next time.'

She smiled back, relieved that he was contemplating a next time. 'It was a beautiful ballet. I'm glad I came.'

Lee reappeared, his face aglow with satisfaction as he waved a stream of waiters to the table. Dish after dish was laid down, six in all, plus various condiments and exquisitely patterned plates of the finest china. He himself produced cutlery of intricately wrought silver.

'You see? I remember. No chopsticks.'

Richard laughed in appreciation. 'You are the perfect host, Lee. Thank you very much. This all looks quite marvellous but, please, don't be offended if we can't eat everything. You've given us a banquet not a supper.'

Lee waved his hands in quick negation. 'No, no. It's all for you to taste. A little bit of this and that. For your pleasure.' He smilingly bowed himself away, leaving his honoured guests hopelessly overwhelmed by his hospitality.

Richard shook his head at Molly. 'I hope you've got a good appetite.'

She grinned. 'I was about to say the same to you.'

'Well, we've got to at least try it all so please help yourself.'

Molly put a spoonful from each dish on to her plate. Richard did the same. They both sighed over how much was still left in the dishes, looked helplessly at each other, then determinedly attacked the food on their plates.

'Mmm! The crab's delicious. I'll manage a second helping of that later,' Molly commented.

'I can recommend the chicken with lemon and almonds, too,' Richard said cheerfully.

All the food was superb, each dish delicately and distinctively flavoured. It was no hardship to do it justice, and when their appetites were completely sated, they sat back with the double pleasure of having eaten well and made Lee happy.

He had the table cleared and served them with tea in the most beautiful teacups Molly had ever seen. So fine was the china it was almost transparent. The tea itself was very fragrant and, although strange to her palate, quite pleasant after the first few sips.

All throughout their meal Richard had plied Molly with questions about Dial-A-Dinner-Party, and she had explained how it worked and how they had gradually built it into a steady business. He had shown a keen interest in the organisation behind it.

'You have a good business head,' he remarked admiringly as they relaxed over their tea.

'Don't credit me with everything. It's Beth who does the accounting.'

'But it was your initiative and enterprise that set up the business.'

Molly shrugged. 'I don't know. I suppose I had the initial idea but then Beth had plenty to add to it. She's really the driving force now. To me it's just a job for which I have the training.'

'Not your life's work?' Richard asked casually.

'I hope not,' Molly sighed, and then smiled. 'I would like to think that life has more to offer than cooking elaborate meals.'

A satisfied little smile played around his lips as he dropped his eyelids and idly pushed the little teacup around its saucer. 'I thought perhaps you might be a career-oriented person.'

'Oh, why?'

He shrugged. 'You're twenty-six. From what you've told me I gather you've been fairly single-minded at making the business work.'

'I had nothing else to do,' she replied with simple honesty.

He raised quizzical, searching eyes. 'Molly,

you're a beautiful woman. You could attract any number of men. Why weren't you married long ago?'

She flushed and fiddled with her own teacup. 'I guess . . . I guess I don't attract the right kind of man.'

'What about when you were younger?' he asked softly.

She took a deep breath, and not even questioning why she should confide in him, proceeded to do so, quite naturally, drawn on by his sympathetic air. 'There was a man when I was in Paris. I suppose you could say I had an affair with him, but I didn't think of it as an affair. I thought it was . . . I thought we were going to be married, but that idea was only in my mind, not his. The reality of the situation was impossible to accept once the rude awakening came.'

She gave a bleak little smile. 'I was very innocent about people in those days. In fact, it's still a fault of mine, believing that people mean what they say.'

'Some do,' he murmured.

Her eyes probed his sincerity for a moment and then dropped. She heaved a sigh and continued. 'When I came home . . . well, I guess I felt rather wary of forming relationships so I worked hard and lived my own little life. Then when Beth's husband ran out on her, she needed help and support. I couldn't walk away, too. She'd been a good friend to me all year and she just fell apart.'

She lifted her gaze to see him nod with understanding. Encouraged, she explained further. 'Dial-A-Dinner-Party was more to get

Beth back on her feet than to set me up in
business, but it consumed all our time. I finally
insisted on having a break from it and it was
while I was on holiday that I met Jeremy. You
know how and why that ended. So there you have
it,' she finished wryly.

The silence which followed was oppressive to
Molly. Again Richard's expression held the
shuttered look which her previous mention of
Jeremy had evoked. Disappointment dragged at
her heart. She suspected that she had just
destroyed any chance of retaining Richard
Pembroke's interest. Confessions might be good
for the soul but they didn't exactly boost a
person's image nor place one in a flattering light.
Honesty could be carried too far, and yet ...
what was the use of pretending some other
background?

She was what she was, and what had been
could not be undone. It was all part of her and if
Richard did not like what he had heard then now
was the time for him to walk away. After all, she
was only human and she did not want an
involvement with a man who could not accept
that she had made mistakes.

'There's no such thing as a new beginning, is
there?' she remarked bitterly, a dull sheen of
mockery veiling the hurt in her eyes.

'I'm sorry?' Her words had obviously drawn
him from deep thought.

She sighed. 'I said there's really no such thing
as a new beginning.'

'There is if you want it enough,' he replied
sharply, then gentled his tone. 'You've been

unlucky, Molly. It's one of the sad ironies of life that the innocent get taken. They're natural victims. Having no guile themselves, they don't recognise it in others.'

'Well, I don't intend to get taken again,' Molly retorted with hard determination, and the defiant warning in her eyes was a direct message for him.

'I'm not a taker, Molly. I don't expect you to believe that but . . . you say you have Sundays free. Will you spend this Sunday with me?'

Relief poured through her and, despite her bitter scepticism of a few moments ago, she did believe him. She told herself that she was still a naïve, stupid fool to give her trust to any man, but everything within her responded to that steady, grey gaze. 'Yes, I will,' she said without hesitation.

A happy grin spread across his face, making him look considerably younger than his years. 'What would you like to do? Get away from the city? A trip up to the Blue Mountains perhaps.'

'That would be pleasant,' she agreed, trying to keep her eagerness from being too obvious. Slowly, slowly, she cautioned herself.

'Would nine o'clock be too early for you?'

'No.'

'Good.' His voice held a rich satisfaction. 'No point in wasting time.'

The comment niggled at the edge of her pleasure. Wasting time for what? Did he think, because she had told him about Philippe, that she could be rushed into his bed? What did he have in mind? 'Why does a QC want to know a cook?' she demanded, almost accusingly.

He laughed, his eyes alight with amusement. 'Well, I wouldn't downgrade the cook part for a start. You're probably a finer cook than I am a QC. And difficult though it is to disregard your talent with *haute cuisine*, that had nothing to do with my desire for your company. Quite simply, I like talking to you, being with you. I find you a very interesting woman. And I'd take it kindly if you'd push aside the QC label and simply view me as an amiable person.'

'Amiable,' she echoed with a smile. It seemed a weak word to apply to Richard Pembroke, yet it did describe his manner to her tonight; kind, friendly, agreeable.

'Do I detect some amusement at that term?' he asked, one eyebrow raised in quizzical mockery.

She laughed and shook her head.

Lee picked that moment to reappear. 'Ah, you are enjoying yourselves,' he beamed. 'May I serve you more tea or wine?'

'No, thank you, Lee. It's time we were going. We've enjoyed ourselves immensely. Miss Fitzgerald is a professional chef herself and she was most impressed with everything you served us.'

'A wonderful supper,' Molly smiled.

Lee was almost beside himself with delight. He bowed them out of the restaurant with much protestation that Mr Pembroke should avail himself of everything Lee could offer more frequently, and please return soon.

Once outside, Richard took possession of Molly's arm and she shot him an amused look.

'What does it feel like to be regarded as God?'

'Embarrassing!' he retorted with feeling.

She laughed up at him, unconsciously resting her head against his shoulder as she did so.

He glanced down at her and the dancing warmth in his eyes suddenly flared into something more intense then amusement. No! her mind screeched. Her head jerked up and she looked sharply away. Not that! Not this soon! No! There had barely been a falter in their step and Richard kept on walking as if there had never been that moment of temptation.

Molly's inner turmoil subsided. They arrived at her car. Richard took the key from her and unlocked the door to the driver's seat. The small car park was empty but for one other car. It was a Porsche.

'Yours?' she nodded.

'Mmm. An extravagant toy.' His mouth curled sardonically. 'One tends to indulge oneself when there's no one else to indulge.'

She looked at her modest Datsun and shrugged. 'I'd probably do the same if I had the means.' She held out her hand. 'Thank you, Richard.'

Strong fingers encased hers and pressed lightly. His eyes probed hers keenly for a moment but her guard was up and there was nothing but politeness to see. 'I'll look forward to Sunday. Good night, Molly.'

'Good night,' she echoed softly and stepped into her car, breaking contact before he should have any other ideas.

He watched her drive off. She saw him in the rear-view mirror, just standing there, looking after her, not making one move towards his own car while she was still in sight.

She drove home slowly, feeling distinctly at odds with herself. Why had she instinctively shied away from giving Richard any chance to kiss her? She had let any number of men kiss her on a first date, men who had not attracted her nearly so much. He could so easily have interpreted her abrupt rejection of the idea as a rejection of him, and that was the last thing she wanted him to think. Far from rejecting him she wanted to know him . . . intimately.

And that was the problem. Intimately. In her innocence she had been easily seduced by Philippe, and her need for love could very well have landed her in Jeremy's bed. She did not want to be persuaded into Richard's bed, not by her own needs or his, not until she was sure it formed a commitment of love.

A kiss was only the first step along the path of sexuality, but she suspected that the path could be taken at an alarming rate by Richard Pembroke. He had wasted no time tonight in bending her to his will, although self-honesty forced Molly to admit that she had been more than pliable. But a man who could affect her physically by a look or a word was a man who could draw an immeasurable response . . . if she let him. And it was too soon for that. She had to know more. Be sure.

A hysterical little laugh bubbled out of her throat. Lord above! She had gone off to the ballet without another thought but to enjoy the performance, and here she was on her way home, plunged into the most serious and far-reaching consequences of knowing a man. A man who could be the most important man in her life. If she was lucky.

CHAPTER SEVEN

THE roses arrived late in the afternoon. The girl who delivered them did so with a funny look at Molly. The eyes were sharp with speculative interest and the mouth seemed to be fighting a grin.

'These were ordered for you this morning, Miss Fitzgerald, but florists don't normally stock this particular type so we had to have them flown in for you. The gentleman's gone to a lot of expense so we hope the delay hasn't caused more trouble.'

Molly looked her bewilderment. 'No. No trouble. Thank you.'

The grin won. 'I'd forgive him if I were you,' the girl declared as she nodded goodbye.

Molly closed the door and stared down at the box in some bemusement. The flowers had to be from Richard. There was no other man in her life. But she could not imagine what the girl was referring to.

'Who was it?' Beth called from the kitchen.

'Florist,' Molly called back.

'Florist?'

Molly took the lid off and parted the tissue paper as she walked down the hall. Some of the roses were only buds, tightly furled yellow petals with crimson tips, but some were fully opened and they were beautiful with their yellow centres

94

graduating to the pink outer petals. Their fragrance was strong and delightful.

'Do you know what these roses are called, Beth?' she asked, placing the box on the kitchen table while she sought a vase.

'Roses!' Gina exclaimed excitedly. 'Oh, he must love you!'

Molly had told them both what had transpired at the ballet and Gina had been gushing romance all day.

'They're called "Peace",' Beth supplied drily. 'At least, that's their common name.'

The speculation which the order had obviously aroused at the florist's shop was now clear and Molly burst out laughing. They had probably envisaged a monumental quarrel with the buyer desperate to make amends, whereas Richard had surely acted on a mere whim, reinforcing his comment on *War and Peace*.

'You can laugh, Molly Fitzgerald,' Beth said with a knowing look. 'But if you ask me, this proves my point. That man is out to undermine your defences, and he's not wasting any time. You watch him!'

While the cautious part of Molly's mind found agreement with Beth, the rest of her filled with pleasure at the gift. Not only were the roses beautiful but the thought behind them reassured her of Richard's interest. It was not until she had lifted them out of the box and into a vase that she found the sealed envelope.

'Ooh! A love-letter too!' Gina crooned excitedly.

'Hardly!' Molly shot at her but she ripped the

envelope open with a delicious feeling of
anticipation.

I had this unshakeable doubt that you might
entertain second thoughts. Please don't. Thank
you again for last night. I look forward to the
pleasure of your company on Sunday.

Richard

'If you have to wear a fatuous smile, you'd better
tell us what's in it,' Beth said in mock disgust.

'Oh, nothing much,' Molly answered airily.
'Just a reminder of our date on Sunday.'

'Some reminder!' Beth scoffed. 'He'll be
expecting a return on his money.'

'Don't believe her, Molly. It's a gesture from
the heart,' Gina insisted.

Molly hoped Gina was right but Beth's words
struck a chord of wariness which continued to
pulse despite the joyous beat of her heart.

On Sunday morning Molly was in a fever of
indecision over what to wear. Feminine vanity
pulled her towards a dress or a pretty skirt but
finally her practical side insisted on jeans. The
temperature was always cooler in the mountains
and if they went on any scenic walks a skirt might
be inhibiting. Her blue and green silk shirt added
some class to an outfit which was completed by
the denim battle jacket. Molly felt reasonably
pleased with her appearance by the time she had
applied a light make-up to her face and brushed
her hair to a shining ripple of waves.

She idly wondered what Richard would look
like in casual clothes, if he would lose a little of
the distinction which formal clothes had em-

phasised. A smile curved her mouth as she pictured him in the wig and gown that barristers wore in court ... very austere and formidable, she decided.

But there was nothing formidable about the man who arrived on the dot of nine o'clock. Except his physical impact. The form-fitting, blue knit shirt and stretch jeans revealed a very masculine physique which had been somewhat neutralised by tailored suits. The face which she had once thought cruel, and then distinctive, was stunningly attractive, wearing as it did a smile which instantly aroused a flock of butterflies in Molly's stomach.

'It's a beautiful morning,' he said by way of greeting.

'Yes. I'm ready to go,' Molly replied stiffly, thinking she was far too vulnerable to physical charm and she was not going to fall into that superficial trap with Richard Pembroke.

His smile turned into a grin. 'I do like punctuality.'

'It's only good manners,' she retorted drily, not wanting him to think she had been counting the minutes for him to come. He needn't start making any assumptions at all.

'I like good manners, too.'

He took her hand, assuming possession of it quite naturally, and Molly fought a battle with herself all the way to the car. Hand-holding could hardly be considered forward. It was friendly. Except her whole body seemed to be affected by the warm touch of those strong fingers. And that wasn't what she wanted. She was not, definitely not, going to be rushed into a physical relationship.

It was a relief to her when Richard held the passenger door open and she could break the contact. She sank into the low-slung luxury of the Porsche and rubbed at the tingling hand in agitated defence. She watched him round the bonnet of the car with the confident stride of a man who was used to getting his own way.

Well, he wasn't going to run this relationship, she thought stubbornly. He had claimed that he wanted her company, that he liked being with her, talking to her, and she was happy to go along with that, but anything physical could wait until she was sure he was not merely attracted to her sexually.

As Richard slid in behind the driver's wheel, Molly met the smiling grey eyes with a cool wariness. The smile faded. His mouth took on an ironic twist.

'You are having second thoughts, aren't you? Are you prepared to chance it or do you want to call the day off?'

A self-conscious blush fanned its heat across her cheeks. 'Why should you think that?' she asked with forced lightness.

His hand reached out as if to touch a burning cheek but she shrank back, resenting the casual intimacy. He turned the movement into a gesture of appeal.

'Is it because I'm Jeremy's brother-in-law?'

Her cheeks flamed even more hotly. 'I'd prefer not to talk about Jeremy,' she said curtly, then with her eyes flaring a defensive challenge, added, 'Do you want to change your mind?'

'Oh no. You've been on my mind ever since we first met. One way or another. I'd hate to see you walk away now,' he replied with a softness which completely disarmed her.

'I'm sorry,' she said impulsively and sent him a tentative smile. 'I didn't mean to be so prickly. I've really been looking forward to going out with you today. And thank you for the lovely roses. They weren't necessary, but thank you.'

His answering smile was warm. 'They made me feel better. I wanted to call you but telephones are hopelessly impersonal, and the truth is, I've never felt so damned unsure of myself with a woman before.'

'You! Unsure!'

'Well, what can you expect after the way you dressed me down?' He threw her a teasing grin as he turned the ignition on. The engine throbbed into powerful life and the car surged forward at the first touch of acceleration. 'You don't know what it's been like. Every morning I've accosted my image in the mirror, stripping it of ego, watching out for puffs of self-righteousness and flattening them, doing eye exercises to ward off blindness . . .'

'A likely story,' Molly scoffed, but she was amused by his assertions.

An eyebrow was lowered in reproach. 'You just don't realise how deep an influence you've had on me.'

Molly grinned. 'I still don't believe a word of it.'

'Ah, you're a hard woman. You dealt me a lesson in humility and just to prove how much

I've taken it to heart, I'm driving you up to the mountains today to show you the work of my humble ancestor.'

'What work?'

'Stone laid on stone. The first road to the inland. My great-great-great-great-grandfather helped to build it, persuaded along by a flogging or two.'

'He was a convict?'

'Yes, poor, unfortunate wretch. Abominable conditions they lived under.' He flashed her a look of sardonic amusement. 'The Pembroke blood might flow beneath silk now, but in 1814 it flowed beneath the lash. And you know what he was transported for?'

'Stealing a loaf of bread?' Molly suggested.

Richard shook his head. 'That I could understand. But what do you think of a handkerchief, a pair of shoes and a prayer book?'

'A prayer book?' Molly echoed in amazement.

'Boggles the mind, doesn't it?' He threw her a grin. 'Now, if it had been a Bible he could have used it to swear his innocence by.'

'How many years did he get?'

'Convicted to be transported to the penal colony of New South Wales, there to do hard labour for a period of seven years,' Richard intoned with mock solemnity.

'Well, I can beat that,' Molly said smugly. 'You English got off easy compared to the Irish. We Fitzgeralds were transported for life, and that without even being brought to trial. Just bundled off to the transport ships while released on bail.'

That raised Richard's eyebrows. 'Got a few

convicts in the skeleton cupboard yourself, have you?'

She grinned triumphantly at him. 'Dyed-in-the-wool rebels. Much more colourful than a thief. They burned Dublin Castle and, not content with rebelling in Ireland, they got out here and rebelled against the New South Wales Government. One of them was hanged for the Castle Hill uprising in 1804.'

'Hmm ... now I know where the fiery spirit comes from.'

Molly laughed and Richard sent her a look of warm satisfaction. 'Tell me more,' he invited.

'That was my father's side. My mother's line traces back to a Mary O'Connor who was transported in 1808. The story goes that she made it difficult for the prosecutor to give her in charge because she bit his wrist, cut his head, tore his shirt, and blacked one of his eyes,' Molly recited with relish.

'Good God! What was she convicted for?'

'Arson.'

Richard roared with laughter.

'Well, the landlord had burned her out of her home so she was only paying him back.'

'That'd be right,' Richard agreed, then in an execrable Irish accent and a spark of devilment in his eyes he added, 'Oh, it's a fine pedigree you've got for yourself, Molly Fitzgerald.'

She laughed and teased back, 'Better than thieves. At least my lot were fighting for their rights.'

'Ah, but you forget the prayer book. My fellow was definitely a holy thief.'

They bantered on with increasing frivolity all the way up the mountains, with Richard drawing Molly out about her family, right up to the present day. He stopped the car in a lay-by on one section of the road to point out its stone foundations, laid by the convicts so long ago. Molly eagerly agreed to his suggestion that they drive as far as Hartley on the other side of Mount Victoria.

Hartley was a historic village where pioneer travellers rested before or after crossing the mountains. Its old stone courthouse virtually invited tourists to step into a bygone era. WANTED posters for runaway convicts hung on the walls and all the relics of justice as it was then dispensed were on display. Molly sat in the dock in the courtroom while Richard took over the Judge's Bench and they fooled around with a mock trial until another visitor wandered in and looked askance at them.

Still laughing over the incident, they returned to the car and drove back to the Hydro-Majestic Hotel near Katoomba. This had been the most fashionable tourist mecca at the turn of the century and the massive complex was still impressive, perched as it was on a cliff edge overlooking the valleys and peaks of the Blue Mountains. They lunched in the old-world splendour of the dining room and afterwards took a stately promenade under the wisteria-covered trellises which protected the paths laid out for guests.

Molly had accepted Richard's arm for the walk without any apprehension, comfortable with the mood of re-living the distant past and completely relaxed after a large meal and a couple of glasses of wine. Richard's whimsical humour had surprised and delighted her and she was enjoying his company immensely.

She realised that he had deliberately set out to dispel the tension between them, but that only increased Molly's appreciation of the man. He cared enough to want her at ease with him and Molly had been only too eager to co-operate. The outing had been everything she could have wished.

They paused at one of the archways to take in the vista of unlimited blue. 'I wonder how many times those early explorers despaired of finding a route through,' she mused.

'With a promise of a thousand acres apiece from Governor Macquarie I doubt they ever despaired,' was the sardonic reply from Richard.

She looked up at him curiously. 'How come you know so much about early Australian history?'

He smiled. 'It's all bound up with the law. How about you?'

'Well, since my dad was a history teacher, bedtime stories mainly dealt with convicts and settlers.'

'Didn't that give you nightmares? No, don't tell me ... you and your brother were blood-thirsty little monsters who lapped up all the horrors.'

Molly grinned. 'Terrific stuff! Much better than Snow White or Cinderella. We never played cowboys and indians or doctors and nurses. It was always red-coats and convicts.'

His eyes crinkled in amusement. 'I bet you were always flouting authority. A right little rebel all down the line.'

'True,' she admitted, her eyes dancing back at him.

His gaze dropped to her mouth. Molly's heart caught. Every nerve in her body tingled alarm. He was going to kiss her and everything would change. It would not be light-hearted fun any more. There would be tension and pressure and emotional havoc, and she didn't want to cope with it. Not yet. Not yet. Not when it had all been so good. Sheer panic jerked her head around. Her eyes fastened on a garden bench.

'Let's sit down over there,' she babbled, already pulling away from him as she pointed.

Her mind was in a hideous whirl, agonising over his silence, pricklingly aware that he had been reluctant to follow her suggestion, cursing herself for reacting like a skittish idiot. The least she could have done was turn the moment aside gracefully instead of bucking like a gauche teenager. He sat down beside her, saying nothing. Tortuous thoughts kept circling her brain until his silence was unbearable.

'It really is a superb view from here,' she rattled out in a high, tinny voice, then could have choked herself for the inanity.

'Yes, it certainly is that,' came the slow, very dry reply.

Oh God! Now I've spoilt it. I've gone and spoilt it all, Molly worried frantically. I've put him off well and truly. What will I do? What can I say to fix it?

'Molly, I have to fly to Melbourne tonight...'

The flat statement jangled in her ears like a death knell to a relationship which could have promised so much if she had given him what he wanted. Would one little kiss have hurt her, disappointment cried. But instinct insisted that it wouldn't have been one little kiss.

'I've been briefed on a case which will probably drag on for three or four weeks,' Richard continued.

She had to show interest, try to recapture something of what they'd had. Her mouth was dry. She quickly worked some moisture into it. 'Is it a murder trial?' She darted a glance at him. His expression was shuttered, telling her nothing of what he was thinking or feeling.

'No, it's one of those fact-finding commissions into corruption that rarely result in anything conclusive. I'm holding a watching brief for a client who's caught up in it. He'll probably have to appear to clear his name, if that's possible.'

'Is he innocent?'

Richard flashed her a wry glance. 'There are degrees of innocence. He doesn't deserve to be ruined.' He heaved a sigh and looked directly at her, his eyes sharply searching. 'Molly, I've enjoyed today very much. I hope you have too...'

'Oh, I have. It's been marvellous,' she almost gushed, hoping against hope that it wasn't the end. She could not hold his gaze for fear of revealing her inner turmoil. Either she was about to receive a brush-off or...

'Would you keep next Sunday free for me if I fly home for it?'

Relief poured through her. He really did want her company. He hadn't been put off. It wasn't just sex he was after. She turned to him with a brilliant smile. 'Of course I will.'

The guarded look dropped from his face. He returned her smile. 'And the next and the next?'

'That's a lot of flying inter-state,' she said, but her eyes glowed with happy anticipation.

'It's only a couple of hours each way. It'll be something for me to look forward to each week. What shall we do next Sunday? Would you like a cruise down the Hawkesbury River?' His eyes were sparkling and there was definitely an eager note in his voice.

'I'd love it,' Molly said with undisguised pleasure. 'Do you own a boat?'

'No, but I can easily hire one at Brooklyn.'

'Does it cost much?' she asked worriedly. It was going to cost him plenty for the air fare each week. She did not want to be an expensive date on top of that.

'I don't care what it costs,' he said extravagantly. 'That's what we'll do.'

'I'll bring lunch. You must let me contribute something.'

'It's a deal,' he declared, and they grinned at each other in mutual delight.

The rest of the afternoon held the added joy of being part of a continuation instead of an end. There was a sweet contentment in Molly's soul, even when Richard had driven her home and escorted her to the front door. Even more so when he let go her hand and showed no intention of kissing her goodbye. The caress of his eyes was enough.

'Could we make an earlier start next Sunday?' he asked.

'What time?'

'Eight o'clock?'

'I'll be ready. And thank you for a wonderful day, Richard.'

'Thank you,' he said softly, and left her with a smile which stayed with her all week.

Their day on the Hawkesbury River was equally wonderful, full of laughter and easy companionship. They cast fishing lines from the boat and caught a bucketful of bream, with Molly triumphant because the largest fish had been her catch. Richard scoffed about beginner's luck but he really seemed pleased for her to be happy. Never had Molly been so relaxed with a man as she was with Richard.

She found him even more physically attractive in shorts and T-shirt. She could not help her gaze lingering occasionally on the strong muscularity of his arms and legs, the taut stomach, the breadth of his chest, and she wondered how it would feel to be in his embrace. The thought excited her but the very strength of that excitement also disturbed her.

Richard did not embrace her. He kept a careful distance between them and whenever he did touch her, there was no hint of sexual intent in the contact. Yet Molly was aware of a determined control in force. It was not that Richard had no desire for her. The fleeting moments of tensions told her he was holding his desire in check. Molly pretended not to notice these moments because she was happy with the way their relationship was going. It suited her to postpone the sexual element which would inevitably force her into a decision she was not ready to make.

On the third Sunday Richard took Molly to the Berowra Waters Inn for lunch. The restaurant was reputed to be one of the best in Australia. Its situation was very picturesque, built on a rather exclusive anchorage and only accessible by launch. The food was excellent and Richard's company was all Molly could wish.

She insisted that their fourth outing be a picnic that she would provide. Richard drove her out to the parkland around Wiseman's Ferry where they could relax on the bank of the river and watch the water-skiers in action. It was a balmy day and they picnicked at leisure. Richard looked tired and Molly ordered him to stretch out on the rug and have a nap, insisting that she was quite happy to sit and watch the skill of the skiers.

'I have so little time with you I don't want to sleep,' he demurred.

'Richard, please. I feel guilty as it is with your having to fly back to Sydney just to take me out. Will your case be over this week?'

'Yes. Two or three more days should see it wound up. Why do you feel guilty? I'm doing what I want to do.'

He had stretched out but he was still propped up on one elbow, slightly behind her. His question was a difficult one to answer and Molly brooded over it without turning around to him. The featherlight caress on her arm startled her.

She shrugged off the shivery feeling and darted questioning eyes at Richard.

He had dropped his hand. His face held a tense watchfulness as he softly asked, 'Still too soon, Molly?'

She knew what he was asking and the physical awareness she had tried to contain could not be contained any longer. 'Richard, it's not that I . . .' She hesitated, feeling intensely vulnerable now that the question was out in the open.

Richard gently tugged her arm. 'Come down here with me. I'm not going to bite. I simply want you to stop hiding from me.'

She felt hopelessly stiff and awkward but she complied with his request. 'I haven't been hiding from you,' she denied, although even as she spoke her lashes veiled the emotional confusion which would be mirrored in her eyes.

'Molly . . .' he chided softly and the brush of fingertips on her cheek forced her to meet his gaze. Doubt and fear clouded the desire in her heart. The grey eyes probed the cloud. 'I want to touch you, kiss you, hold you in my arms. You must know that. Yet you keep shying away at the mere suggestion of any little intimacy. Be honest with me now. Is there no chance of your sharing that feeling?'

Shame burnt into her cheeks. He had been very patient with her and she had taken all his attentions without giving him the encouragement he needed to feel. 'I'm sorry. I have been mean,' she mumbled.

'No. I didn't expect sexual payment,' he said quietly. 'But I don't want our relationship to remain platonic either. So what now, Molly? Are we going anywhere?'

'If . . . if you want to,' she choked out over her uncertainty.

His eyes softly mocked her answer. 'Do you want to? That's the question.'

'Yes,' she whispered, hoping against hope that the direction he meant was towards marriage because there was no doubt in her mind now that she was very close to loving this man.

He leaned over and kissed her before she had time for any thought of protest. One hand cradled her head as he lowered her shoulders to the rug and not for a moment did his mouth leave hers, tantalisingly soft, sweetly persuasive, and the desire to give in to its persuasion was too compelling to resist. The deep well of feeling which Molly had guarded, broke through her defensive barriers and she kissed Richard back with a fervour which caught him by surprise.

She felt his hesitation, and then the restraint he had held on himself dissolved, giving way to a passionate possession of all she was willing to offer. His fingers threaded her head with pressing urgency. One of her breasts was crushed under a wildly thumping heart as his chest half-covered hers. Molly clutched him tightly to her, uncaring of his weight, uncaring of anything but the rampant desire which begged for satisfaction.

He left her mouth throbbing with sensitivity. His warm breath fanned her cheek in uneven gasps. 'Molly . . . is this for me? . . . For me?' he repeated incredulously.

She opened eyes which held no guile, no veil of pretence, but a limpid reflection of the feeling which consumed her. She did not understand his question. She simply looked up at him wondering why there was a strained line to his face, a doubt in his eyes. What more assurance did he need than what she had given him so unreservedly?

He expelled a sigh and his eyes suddenly held a melting tenderness. 'Why did I wait so long?' he mused, softly stroking the hair away from her temples.

She sensed that he was about to kiss her again and she panicked. 'Richard . . .'

'Mmm?' His mouth was closer.

'Richard . . .' The question fretting at the edge of her mind had to be voiced before she relinquished control. 'I don't want an affair with you.' The words were a husky croak, scraping over a huge lump of emotion and her eyes begged a denial from him.

He frowned. 'Precisely what are you saying, Molly. Spell it out.'

She sighed and dragged the old scars into the light. 'I've been supposedly loved by two men, Richard. I believed both of them. But they didn't love me. They didn't care what happened to me. All they cared about was getting what they wanted from me.' She sucked in a quick breath and spelled it out. 'I know you want me. And I . . . I like you very much. I've liked being with you. Which is why I've held back from . . . from encouraging you beyond friendship. Because I didn't want it to end. But if it's an affair you want, then it ends now. Today. Before I get any more deeply involved with you. So please . . . be honest with me.'

He heaved a sigh and rolled on to his back, separating himself from her in an action so abrupt that it struck a chill in Molly's heart. His hands were tucked under his head and his narrowed gaze seemed fixed on the river. His silence was too great a weight to bear. Molly stirred herself and sat up, turning her back on him so that she did not have to see the decision on his face. She plucked a blade of grass and shredded it with trembling fingers.

'I did warn you. That first night,' she muttered miserably.

'There is such a thing as mutual desire, Molly. It's not a take. It's giving and receiving,' he stated quietly.

There was nothing she could say to that. She simply did not want sex without commitment, no matter how he argued the case.

'I do want you,' he said bluntly. 'I thought, when you kissed me back, you wanted me. I can't stop myself from wanting you. I can't snap my fingers and make the feeling fade away. I can control it but I don't see why I have to if you want me, too. I'm not asking you to rush into bed with me, Molly. I'm not asking you to have an affair with me. Just to respond honestly to me so I know where the hell I am with you. You had me thinking I was a bloody neuter in your eyes.'

The muted frustration in his voice made her squirm. 'I'm sorry. I didn't mean to make you feel that. I just didn't want to be pressured,' she explained desperately. 'All right,' he said after a long pause. 'I can understand that. But what do you expect of me now, Molly? Am I supposed to propose marriage before I'm allowed near you again?'

Put like that she knew her attitude was unreasonable, hopelessly unreasonable. But she also knew herself to be hopelessly vulnerable to his lovemaking and she was frightened of being hurt again. On the other hand, it was clear that if she did not put herself at risk, there was no hope at all for any future with Richard. Tears of despair stung her eyes as she made her decision.

'No . . .' She swallowed hard in an effort to keep her distress from showing. 'No. You don't have to do that.'

Again there was an excruciating silence. A hand touched her shoulder, curled around it, took hold. She shivered. It gently kneaded the soft flesh. What little resistance Molly had melted into limp futility. She wanted Richard. Maybe she even loved him. Whatever happened she wanted to go on seeing him.

'Molly, I don't want to talk to your back,' he said softly.

She blinked hard to force away the tears and slowly swung down to his level, propped on one elbow.

He reached out and forcibly tilted her chin. 'Look at me, Molly.'

She lifted her heavy lashes and looked into sympathetic eyes.

'I know you've been hurt. I can't turn back the clock and take the hurt away. I can't turn the clock forward and tell you the future. I don't know if there's a future for us together. I was certainly beginning to doubt it until you showed me a response a few minutes ago. A lot depends on you, Molly. I need your trust. We can't go far without it. Will you spend next Sunday with me at my home?'

At his home. In his bedroom? Molly rejected the thought as unfair even as it formed. Richard had been completely open with her. There was no deceit. She had no reason to distrust him. His request was reasonable.

'All right,' she agreed.

The hand under her chin slid around to cup her cheek. It paused there for a moment. Molly's insides turned to jelly, a mass of quivering anticipation. The hand dropped away.

'That's fine.' Richard gave her an encouraging smile. 'Now we're getting somewhere.'

He did not kiss her again. He told her about his home, a renovated terrace house at Woolhara. Gradually Molly's emotional tension eased and by the end of the afternoon she was relaxed enough to be able to talk quite naturally. She even laughed. Richard made the drive home as pleasant as any other drive had been. As usual he escorted Molly to her front door and she thanked him for a lovely day.

'Next week we'll swim and laze by the pool and I'll cook you a barbecue lunch,' he said matter-of-factly.

'That sounds great,' she said with a smile of relief. No bedrooms. Richard had told her that his swimming-pool virtually filled the pocket-handkerchief back garden, and, since the adjoining terrace houses overlooked it, he could hardly be envisaging a full-scale seduction there.

'Nine o'clock be all right?'

'Fine,' she nodded.

She did not notice his hand lifting. Suddenly it was sliding under her hair to the nape of her neck and another hand was around her waist, drawing her towards him.

'I don't want a cool little handshake, Molly,' he murmured, and then he was kissing her, moulding the whole length of her body to his, and nothing at all mattered but the warm passion of his mouth and the possessive strength of his embrace and the masculine pressure of his body inviting her pliancy.

Her melting response was totally instinctive and undeniably positive, and Molly had no idea how long the kiss lasted. When it did she felt very shaky indeed.

Richard's smile held immense satisfaction. 'I won't mind going back to Melbourne with that memory. 'Bye, Molly.' He touched her cheek in a farewell salute and strode away, leaving her in a daze of awakened sensuality.

CHAPTER EIGHT

MOLLY had to make a concentrated effort to compose herself before facing Beth. All these weeks she had blithely dismissed her friend's scepticism about relationships, declaring that Richard was a thorough gentleman. Molly assured herself that Richard was still a gentleman, just a more disturbing one.

She could hardly object to his kisses when she had been so responsive to them and he certainly could not be called pushy. And he was right. No relationship could remain static. It had to develop further or it lost interest through lack of stimulus.

She walked into the house all ready to deflect a teasing gibe from Beth, but her entrance did not prompt a greeting. The house was dark and quiet and it felt oddly empty. Molly frowned. It was not like Beth to go out. At this time of the evening she invariably watched the Sunday news programmes on television.

'Beth?' she called tentatively.

There was no answer. It suddenly occurred to Molly that her friend might be suffering one of her occasional migraine headaches. Very quietly she opened the door of Beth's bedroom and peered around it. The huddled figure on the bed seemed to confirm the idea.

'Beth? Are you asleep?' Molly whispered.

'No.' The answer sounded fretful.

'Can I get you anything?'

Silence. Then slowly and awkwardly the figure uncurled itself. Legs straggled over the side of the bed.

'Don't get up, Beth,' Molly protested quickly. 'I'll get you whatever you want.'

Despite the offer, Beth heaved herself up and sat with her head in her hands. 'I'm all right,' she mumbled.

'You don't look all right or sound all right,' Molly said in concern. She switched the light on to satisfy herself on the matter.

'Don't!'

Beth's croak of protest was too late. Molly stared at the tear-blotched face for a long, shocked moment before she had the presence of mind to switch the light off again.

'I'm sorry. I didn't realise. I'm sorry,' she blathered in embarrassment.

'It doesn't matter,' Beth said wearily. 'I need to talk about it anyway and I'm sure to start bawling again. Make us a cup of tea, will you, Molly? I'll go have a wash and tidy up.'

'Sure you're all right?' Molly asked anxiously.

'I'll live,' Beth said wryly. 'Go on.'

Molly felt extremely agitated over Beth's deep depression. Clearly her friend had been crying for hours. Maybe the cause lay in the loneliness of the Sundays which Molly had spent with Richard, or fear over the business should Molly leave it to get married. A horrid feeling of guilt wormed around Molly's heart as she made the tea and popped some bread into the toaster in case Beth had not eaten at all.

Beth came into the kitchen and sat down at the table, slumping forward to lean her head on one hand. The bleak, washed-out look on her face denied any interest in food, but Molly pushed the tea and toast at her.

'Thanks,' Beth mumbled.

Molly sat down and waited on tenterhooks for Beth to confide her problem.

'A man came today,' she said tiredly. 'He gave me a letter from Brendan.'

'Brendan!' Molly gasped. Beth's husband had not even entered her mind as a likely cause of trouble. Two years had pushed him well and truly into the background.

Beth shot her a rueful look. 'Yes, it was a shock to me, too. The man was from New Zealand, over here on holiday. Brendan had asked him to find me, see if I was all right and deliver the letter.'

'Brendan's in New Zealand?'

Beth nodded. 'That's where he went when he ... he ran away. It wasn't another woman, Molly. It was gambling. That's why there was no money left. And there were men after him. Debt-collectors for a bookmaker.'

'But why didn't he tell you?' Molly burst out resentfully. 'Why did he leave you without a word?'

Tears filled Beth's eyes. 'He'd promised me that he'd never gamble again. He'd ... he'd done it before, Molly, but my father bailed us out of trouble and Brendan swore he'd never touch another bet. He said he meant only to use the tips he got in the restaurant, but it's like a fever with him, and of course it soon escalated.'

She sighed despondently. 'It's always the next bet which is going to be the big winner, the one to get him out of trouble and set him straight. Only it didn't happen and he couldn't pay up in time, and he received threats. He thought it was safer for me if I didn't know where he was. And he thought I was better off without him.'

She lifted wry eyes. 'That's just how he would think, Molly. Too guilty to own up and too ashamed to ask me to share his troubles. He was so uptight those last couple of months, all closed up in himself. I wanted to have a child but he wouldn't consider it. I thought it had to be another woman. I just didn't think of gambling. Not after the last time. I was so sure he wouldn't do it again.'

'So what now, Beth? Why did he write?' Molly prompted cautiously.

A painful uncertainty clouded Beth's eyes. 'He . . . he wants . . . he's asking if there's any chance that I'll forgive him.'

'And is there?'

The tears welled up and spilled over. 'I don't know. I don't know. How can I, Molly?' She buried her face in her hands and her shoulders heaved as she fought to contain her sobs. 'Two years . . . it's been two years . . . and so much heartache. I'm better off . . . I'm better off without him.'

Molly waited for the sobs to subside. Her mind roved back over the work-driven existence Beth had led since Brendan had left her. There had been satisfaction in achievement but little else. No love, no warmth, no laughter . . . not happy laughter. Beth was eaten up inside, with nothing left to give to any other man. She would never marry again. She had not even considered getting a divorce since Brendan's desertion. She would never have children. It was not a life at all. It was existence.

'Are you really better off without him, Beth?' she asked when all was quiet.

Beth lifted agonised eyes. 'How can you say that, Molly? You were there.'

'Yes. But before that ... you did love him, Beth. When I first met you both I thought you were a happy couple.'

'But he broke his promise and ran out on me and left me destitute, Molly.'

'I know.' There was no overlooking the terrible thing Brendan had done to a woman he supposedly loved, a wife who had stuck loyally to him through previous troubles.

'How can I ever believe him again?' It was a cry from the soul.

Molly couldn't answer it. 'I don't know, Beth. Maybe you can't. But that doesn't mean you couldn't have some kind of happiness with him. You haven't been happy without him.'

'How could I be happy with him after what he's done?' Beth demanded bitterly.

Molly tried for calm common sense. 'I think it's a matter of balance, Beth. Which life is better ... a life with him or without him?'

It was the decision she herself had made this afternoon, whether to lead a sterile life or risk hurt for the possibility of winning love. Richard had done nothing to hurt her. Indeed, he had indulged her defensiveness. She really had no reason not to trust him.

Beth had every reason in the world not to trust Brendan, and yet ... maybe this time he would keep his promises and they could make a successful go of their marriage. If Beth did not try she would never know, just as if Molly didn't go along with Richard she would never know if their relationship could be made into a lasting one.

Beth heaved a ragged sigh. 'I love him and I hate him, too.' Her mouth twisted in bitter irony. 'But there never was any other man for me. What should I do, Molly?'

'Why not leave the situation open? You could write to him without committing yourself to any decision. Say you're willing to see him and talk. If he wants you he'll come over here and then you can work out how you feel.'

'Yes.' Beth nodded a couple of times. 'Yes, I could do that. If he comes, that'd prove ... well, something, wouldn't it?'

The wretched hope that peered out of Beth's red eyes almost moved Molly to tears. She swallowed hard. 'I guess you don't gain anything if you don't take a chance. If you think it's worth a try, Beth, then go for it,' she advised softly, aware that she herself was making a new resolution.

Beth scraped back her chair and stood up. 'I'll go and write a letter. That's what I'll do. Thanks, Molly.'

For the next few days Beth was so nervy and distracted, Molly worried if the advice she had given had indeed been right, but on Thursday Brendan telephoned from New Zealand and any doubts Molly had entertained were immediately squashed. Beth was suddenly a different person: young, alive, glowing.

'He's flying over here this Saturday, and he's coming to see me on Sunday,' she announced with a fearful happiness which completely belied the hate she had declared only days before.

Until Sunday morning Beth's moods swung from elation to wracking uncertainty, but, come the day, she was like a teenager getting ready for a first date; what to wear, how to look, what to say, how even to greet him. Molly tried to calm her down but it was an impossible task, particularly when Molly herself was preoccupied with getting ready for her day with Richard.

She chose to wear the rather eye-popping outfit she had bought on her holiday at Surfers' Paradise. The wrap-around skirt was geometrically patterned in graduating diamonds of sea-green, royal-blue and violet. The tunic top was thigh length and could be tucked into the skirt or worn by itself as a cover-up for the matching bikini. Molly had been so pleased with the outfit she had bought green sandals to complete it.

At a quarter to nine the doorbell rang.

'Is it Richard?' Beth asked anxiously.

Molly shrugged. 'It's a bit early for him. When are you expecting Brendan?'

'I don't know. I didn't think to make a time. Just this morning.'

'Well, will you answer it or shall I?'

Beth was all of a flutter. 'You, Molly. I . . . I

was just going to put the kettle on.' She turned tail and almost scuttled into the kitchen.

Molly shook her head, wondering if she should leave Beth alone if the caller was Richard. Clearly her friend's courage was teetering. The dilemma was solved as soon as she opened the door. Brendan was on the front porch, seemingly about to drop a bunch of daisies behind the camellia bush.

He turned an agonised face to the door and his relief at seeing Molly was obviously enormous. He was thinner than she remembered. The dapper moustache was gone. The short-sleeved sports shirt revealed forearms which were tanned and sinewy as if he had been doing hard work out of doors. His face was also darkly tanned, weathered, older; still attractive but holding now a maturity which had been lacking before. The two years had not sat easily on Brendan.

'Hello, Molly,' he said nervously. 'Is ... is Beth here?'

'Yes. Inside. Are those daisies for her?'

He jerked in the outstretched arm and looked down at the flowers, his mouth twisting into a grimace. 'I thought ... Beth always liked daisies. But maybe they look cheap.' He lifted eyes which held a frantic anxiety. 'I should've bought roses.'

Molly gave him a sympathetic smile. 'I don't think so, Brendan. It's the thought that counts. Come on in. Beth's just making a pot of tea.'

'I'm not too early?'

'No.' About two years too late, Molly thought wryly, but she did not voice the thought. This meeting was going to be tough enough on both of them.

Still he hesitated. 'I don't know what to say to her, Molly,' he confessed wretchedly.

'You'll think of something. You're here. That says quite a bit by itself. Now, do come in. Beth's waiting.'

She tugged his arm. He stiffened his back and stepped into the hallway.

'Walk straight through,' Molly instructed and raised her voice. 'Beth, it Brendan.'

They came face to face in the living room. Molly did not follow Brendan in but her own anxiety for a happy outcome to this reunion prompted her to check that the first moments were auspicious.

Neither one rushed into speech. Their bodies were tense, faces strained, eyes searching eyes. Tentatively Brendan held out the daisies. His throat worked convulsively but no sound was emitted.

Beth took the flowers. She stared down at them. One hand plucked a petal. Both hands were shaking. She looked up and her eyes were swimming with tears. Her mouth quivered as she spoke. 'You remembered . . .'

'Beth.' The name exploded out of him. 'I . . . Oh God! Don't cry. Please don't cry.'

His arms instinctively reached for her. One step and he was crushing her to him, hands running feverishly over her in a blind attempt to comfort. His own eyes were squeezed shut but tears oozed from their corners and trickled down his cheeks.

Molly turned away. Very quietly she collected her bag from her bedroom and let herself out the front door. She took a deep breath to clear the choked-up feeling in her throat. Richard was alighting from the Porsche. Even with her vision blurred he looked wonderful to Molly, so straight and strong and . . . and dependable.

She raced down the path to meet him. To his startled surprise she flung her arms around his neck and planted a kiss on his cheek. He recovered very quickly, his arms sliding around her in delighted possession. His smile flashed brilliantly until he saw the film of tears in her eyes.

'Hey! You're crying.'

'No, I'm not.' She smiled to prove it. 'I'm just happy.'

'This happy to see me?' he asked incredulously.

'Yes and no.'

He frowned but it was a teasing frown. 'I don't care for that "no" part.'

'Let's get on our way and I'll tell you all about it.'

She started to pull away but he held her fast. 'Now wait a minute. A miracle happens and you expect me to let it go with only a peck on the cheek? Let's do the thing properly.'

And he kissed her on the mouth, very thoroughly, with total disregard for the fact that they were on a public street. Molly's blood raced around her veins and produced a heated flush on her cheeks by the time Richard had decided the occasion had been made memorable enough. His eyes caressed the dewy softness of hers and he touched one burning cheek with a gentle finger.

'Now we'll go,' he said softly, and smiled.

'Yes. I think we should move,' she said dizzily.

He laughed and bundled her into the car, then jogged around the bonnet in his eagerness to join her. He revved the engine with youthful exuberance and they were off.

'Now you can tell me what brought on the very welcome welcome,' he teased.

'Well, I was pleased to see you.'

'I'll take that as proven. And very pleased I am, too.'

She gave a self-conscious laugh but she was too full of emotion to take issue with him about anything. 'I've just witnessed what I hope will be the beginning of a happy ending for Beth and Brendan.'

'Brendan? The husband who deserted?'

Molly nodded. 'But they really do love each other, Richard. It was so touching when he came this morning. It was like a revelation, seeing what love was all about. I can tell you nothing else really mattered but their being together. It was heart-breaking and wonderful at the same time.'

She told him all that had happened since she had arrived home the previous Sunday and Richard listened with the sympathetic air which she found immensely endearing.

'And now you think they'll live happily every after,' he concluded whimsically.

She flashed him a sardonic look. 'I'm not that starry-eyed. I don't imagine everything in the garden will be rosy but I'd say Brendan has been as miserable without Beth as she's been without him. They need each other and they love each other. If Beth has sole management of their finances so that she can feel secure, then I reckon they can make a good go of their marriage.'

'Have you thought how that will affect you?' His gaze flicked to her for a moment, sharply assessing.

'Me?' Molly frowned. 'How do you mean?'

'If Beth goes to New Zealand with Brendan, you'll be left without a partner. This reconciliation is not exactly in your best interests.'

'How can you think that way?' she burst out hotly. 'A business isn't as important as Beth's happiness.'

To her surprise he gave her a warm smile of approval. 'I didn't say it was. I just wondered if you'd thought about how you'll manage.'

'I'll manage,' Molly asserted firmly. 'I always have managed to look after myself. Beth can go off with my blessing and every good wish for her future.'

His smile turned into an appeasing grin. 'I don't doubt you, Molly. What do you think you'll do with Dial-A-Dinner-Party?'

She shrugged. 'I don't know. Take on less commitments, I suppose. I'll still have Gina with me. Whatever happens I'm not likely to starve. There's always a job for a good cook.'

'Mmm. Could do with one myself.' His eyes twinkled mischief at her. 'Do you take live-in jobs?'

'Exclusive rights come at a very high price, Richard Pembroke,' she mocked.

'Well, I'd expect a deduction for fringe benefits,' he said blithely.

'What fringe benefits?'

'The pleasure of working for an employer who appreciates you.'

'Oh? And what form does this appreciation take?'

'I've been having this fantasy . . . thinking how very pleasant it would be to come home each night to a meal cooked by Molly Fitzgerald. Then I've thought how much more pleasant it would be if she sat down and shared it with me. How even more pleasant if she greeted me with a kiss at the door . . . like the way you greeted me this morning. Gives me hope, that does. And it make me think . . .'

'I think you'd better stop thinking,' she blurted out. A hot tide of blood had swept up her throat and spread across her cheeks. His fantasy was a reflection of hers but it had the wrong basis.

He suddenly pulled the car over to the kerb, switched off the ignition, released his seat-belt and was turning towards her before Molly could even question why he had stopped so abruptly. 'You're absolutely right,' he declared with conviction. 'Thinking is not good enough.'

'Richard . . .'

His mouth grazed over hers with tantalising softness.

'It's broad daylight,' she forced out.

'So it is,' he agreed and nibbled teasingly at her lower lip. A hand slid caressingly under her hair. A thumb was lightly exploring the curl of her ear.

Molly's heart was pulsing overtime. She tried one last weak protest. 'Richard . . .'

'I'm here,' he murmured, and kissed her with a

slow sensuality which expelled every other thought but the desire he was so surely evoking.

'If you keep kissing me like that, Molly, I'll end up with a parking fine,' he said with husky provocation.

'I'm not stopping you from . . .' she began, then realised that one of her hands was gripping his head, her fingers firmly entwined in the thick black hair.

The grey eyes laughed at her confusion as she quickly let go. 'I didn't say I minded.'

'You're supposed to be a law-abiding barrister,' she retorted accusingly.

'Ah, but I feel like a new man.' He settled back behind the wheel with a satisfied sigh. 'In fact, I've never felt so alive.'

The verve with which he drove the Porsche the rest of the way to his home certainly demonstrated a light-heartedness which Molly could not feel.

She had suspected all along that once she had given Richard a green light there would be no stopping him. It was useless to pretend to herself that she even wanted to stop him. She wanted him to love her. She wanted his fantasy to come true, but with her in the role of his wife, not a live-in cook. All she could do now was trust him and hope he was indeed a man of honour, because she no longer felt capable of refusing whatever he asked of her.

Molly's thoughts drifted to Beth and for a little while she envied her friend. Despite the trauma of sorting out their differences, despite all the hurt Brendan had given her, there could be no doubt in Beth's mind that Brendan was hers and only hers, and, whatever other faults he had, the constancy of his love was not in question. They were married. They could set up a home together. They could have a family. They had a future.

Molly looked hard at Richard and willed him to envisage a similar future with her.

CHAPTER NINE

RICHARD turned the car into a narrow lane which bisected two rows of terraced houses whose garages backed on to it. The fences were high and certainly not of the same age as the houses. Neither were the garages. Clearly a lot of money had been spent on updating this area of Woolhara. Richard pressed a remote-control device, a door rolled open and he drove the Porsche into a neat, modern garage whose end wall had been fitted out with a row of large storage cupboards. The door behind them closed automatically.

'What do you keep in all those cupboards?' Molly asked in an attempt to cover a ridiculous attack of shyness as Richard helped her out of the car.

'The pool filter, some foldaway outdoor furniture, and a few household tools. Not that I'm much of a handyman, but I have been known to swing a hammer in an emergency. Are you a handywoman?' he asked with a wide grin.

'I can fix a fuse and change a washer in a tap, but if you're looking for a carpenter, you're out of luck,' she retorted lightly.

Once out of the close confinement of the garage Molly could relax. Sunlight bounced off the pool and she shaded her eyes from the glare with one hand. Richard held the other, but the warm pleasure tingling up her arm was within the bounds of her control.

At the far end of the pool a vine-covered pergola ran out from the house and arranged in the shade were two comfortable-looking sun-loungers, separated by a table. To their left was a closed-in area, presumably a utility room, and to the right was a workmanlike portable barbecue.

'Do you do much entertaining, Richard?' she asked curiously.

'Not here. I deal with business at restaurants or clubs. I invite only close friends to my home.'

She slanted him a teasing smile. 'Then I guess I'm honoured.'

He laughed. 'You, I'll even invite into my kitchen,' he said with a flourish as he opened the back door for her.

Molly stepped into a surprisingly spacious area, made more so by the row of windows looking out over the pool. The floor was of a multi-hued slate, colourful in an earthy way. On a large, shaggy rug was set a table and six chairs, softly upholstered in brown leather. A long wooden worktop separated the dining area from the kitchen wall, which was very modern and utilitarian, with every facility efficiently planned into one long unit.

'Very nice,' she commented admiringly.

'Very basic,' was Richard's dry retort. 'It's a very basic bachelor's residence. Two rooms up, two rooms down. Knocking out a few walls was the only way to get a decent amount of natural light into each room. I hate small, dark places.'

'Then what made you choose a terraced house? They're almost always small and dark.'

He grinned. 'This one isn't any more. It has more sense of privacy than an apartment and I wanted my own pool. The position here is close to the city, handy for the law-courts and my chambers. Want to see the front room?'

Molly nodded, slightly apprehensive that he might offer to show her the bedroom next. He led her past the central staircase which she noticed had been given a skylight above the top landing. The living room was very attractive. Brown and beige striped curtains framed the french windows facing the street. Brown leather chesterfields faced each other across a low, wooden coffee table. The thick beige carpet lightened the room and paintings on the walls provided colour. The cupboard and shelf-unit on the staircase wall held a hi-fi, television, books, a large collection of tapes, and various ornamental pieces.

'You've really made yourself a very comfortable home,' Molly remarked appreciatively.

'Mmm ... it gets a bit lonely.'

She looked sharply at him, hoping, fearing, that he might suggest she eliminate his loneliness.

He smiled. 'Come on. I'll get some drinks and we'll go outside and bask in the sun. What would you like?'

'Fruit juice, please,' she replied quickly, not knowing if she was relieved or disappointed that he had not pursued the point.

She followed him back to the kitchen and watched as he loaded a tray with drinks and a dish of nuts. 'Go on out to the changing room and strip off if you like,' he invited off-handedly.

'Yes. All right,' she agreed, knowing that she had to do so sooner or later and that the longer she left it the more self-conscious she would feel. Normally she would not give a second thought to appearing in a bikini but Richard had aroused her physical awareness to an unprecedented level.

The changing-room contained a shower, toilet, vanity-unit, washing-machine, sink and dryer. The lime-green tiling and white fittings achieved a fresh, clean look which made it a pleasant little room. Molly unfastened her skirt and hesitated for a long time before reluctantly removing the tunic top. She took hairpins from her bag and coiled the longer lengths of her hair into a knot above the nape of her neck. She felt very naked both mentally and physically when she finally emerged to join Richard.

He had discarded his shorts and shirt and was in the act of stepping down from the back door, a plate of potato crisps in his hand. His gaze lifted to Molly and to her intense embarrassment he froze in his tracks, his eyes making a slow, appreciative traverse of every curve on her body.

'Please stop it. You're giving me goose-bumps,' she begged in protest.

He shook his head and grinned at her. 'I can't help it. You're so damned beautiful.'

'I am not,' she insisted defensively and strode quickly to the nearest lounger, stretching out on it and wishing there was a sheet to pull over her. 'I'm the same woman you've been seeing for weeks,' she added with forced lightness.

Richard walked over and set the plate of crisps on the table, still looking at her but with a devilish gleam in his eye now. 'Well, let me tell you, as fine as you look in jeans and skirts, clothes don't do you justice, Molly.'

Nor him, she thought as her eyes skated up the powerful thighs, jumped the all-too-suggestive swimming briefs, and followed an intriguing V of sprinkled black curls to an impressive chest before lifting to the grey eyes she had come to love. 'You look pretty super yourself for a law-man,' she said flippantly, trying hard to ignore the wild flutter in her heart.

'Now that incurs a penalty. You can't be allowed to get away with mocking the law, my girl.' He bent down and kissed her nose.

Molly sucked in a quick breath. 'Playing judge again, are you?'

'And that's contempt of court,' he murmured and claimed her mouth.

Molly was so distracted she was unaware of Richard's purpose when he slid his hands up under her arms. Suddenly she was hoisted to her feet and imprisoned in an embrace which had her whole body thrust against his.

She slapped his shoulders and pressed back. 'That's not playing fair, Richard,' she protested in panic.

'But I like it,' he drawled, his eyes simmering with a warmth which sent tingles all over her skin. 'You've been so elusive for so long, Molly Fitzgerald, I have this irresistible urge to prove to myself that I now have solid reality instead of dreams.'

Solid reality! He was that, all right. All hard, strong muscle inviting her to succumb to the temptation of savouring the sheer masculinity of the man. She wanted to run her hands over the broad shoulders, wanted to feel the sensual rub of his chest against her soft skin, wanted to . . . Oh, Lord! She couldn't let herself think that! She had to hold him off until . . .

'Molly . . .'

She lifted eyes which mirrored the conflict between caution and desire.

An indulgent little smile curved his lips. 'Don't worry. I know it's too soon but I couldn't bear another wall of reserve sliding up around you. I want to know what you're thinking, and I want to feel what you're feeling. So let go, Molly. Trust me.'

He softly kissed the doubting eyes shut. With a shuddering little sigh Molly released the weak threads of resistance and offered her mouth to his. He made no passionate demand on it, but rather played at a slow, sweet seduction of her senses, and Molly was entranced by his gentleness. He plotted a leisurely trail of kisses around her face, explored the curl of her ear, the curve of her throat, and returned again and again to her mouth, deepening his possession of it each time until it was Molly who held him there, pleading for the passion he had so far withheld.

One arm tightened around her, pressing her yielding flesh even closer, and his other hand tore through the loosely knotted hair at the back of her head, and there was no more control. A wild elation pulsed through Molly's veins, inciting her to match his primitive savagery without inhibition. She ran her hands over the tense muscles in his back, exulting in the freedom to touch, to hold, to mark as her own.

It excited her further to feel him shudder as she dug her fingers into the small of his back. Then abruptly he released her mouth and roughly pressed her head on to his shoulder. His chest heaved again and again as he drew in deep breaths.

'Molly, this is real, isn't it? It's not just me?' The low huskiness of his voice held a note of strain.

'No. It's not just you,' she sighed, nestling her face into the curve of his neck and kissing the taut muscle there. She wanted to sink into him, belong to him forever.

'You are, without a doubt, the most exciting damned woman I've ever met in my life. Fire and air. And now earth.' He gave an exultant chuckle as he slid his hands up her body to her shoulders and pulled her back enough to look into her face. His eyes held a radiant happness. 'I don't think I could ever have enough of you, Molly, but I guess I'd better go for that fourth element, water, and cool off before I'm tempted further than you want. Come and swim with me?'

'Yes.' The truth was she'd do anything for him but she was grateful for the reprieve, even though her body ached for his. No commitment had yet been made.

He swung her up into his arms as if she was a featherweight, took the few strides to the edge of the pool and jumped in.

'My hair!' Molly squealed as water splashed around her.

'Doesn't matter,' he grinned.

'No, I guess it doesn't,' she grinned back.

He let her go and they swam the length of the pool several times in a leisurely crawl. Richard had been right to force the issue, Molly reflected ruefully. She no longer felt uncomfortable about her body or his. She could look at him with uninhibited pleasure and revel in the way he looked at her. The protective wall she had tried to build around herself had crumbled under his determined assault and, instead of feeling captured, Molly felt a sense of freedom which was wonderfully intoxicating.

She enjoyed the brisk towelling-down he gave her when they climbed out of the pool. He insisted on rubbing the moisture from her hair, which he did so ineptly they both ended up laughing.

'I'll learn,' he promised her and the promise put a glowing hope in Molly's heart, suggesting as it did a long future of intimacy.

They lay on the sun-loungers, sipping drinks, nibbling nuts and crisps and idly discussing a variety of topics which had no importance at all because the real conversation was in their eyes, a hopeful questioning which found joyful answers.

At lunchtime Richard cooked steak and onions on the barbecue and produced a simple salad as an accompaniment, declaring that he could have done something fancier but had decided not to risk inviting Molly's criticism. He staunchly denied her accusation of laziness and teasingly added that she could whip up a dessert if she wasn't satisfied.

Molly was more than satisfied. She loved Richard Pembroke. She loved everything about him; his strength, his gentleness, his compassion, his sense of humour ... the list of his virtues seemed endless and she could find no vice in him at all. In her eyes, he was perfect.

'You know, in all our talking, you've never spoken of your family,' she remarked as the thought struck her. They were back on the loungers, relaxing with their after-dinner coffee, and she threw Richard a questioning look. 'Not your immediate family. I've told you all about mine.'

A frown lowered his eyebrows for a moment and didn't quite clear. 'I thought it might be a sensitive area. There's only my mother and my sister. And her children,' he added with a hint of reluctance.

His sister. Married to Jeremy. Jeremy's children. Molly immediately understood his reticence. On their first Sunday outing she had curtly demanded that he did not speak of Jeremy. A sudden apprehension tied a knot in her stomach. She had almost forgotten Jeremy and he meant absolutely nothing to her now, but would the brief connection with him form an impediment to her sharing a life with Richard? It would certainly make a meeting with Richard's sister extremely awkward. But Jeremy and Dana lived in Brisbane, she argued defensively. And she had nothing to feel guilty about. She had not been the party at fault. All the same, the sensible thing would be to talk about it now. Get it out in the open.

'Your sister must be younger than you,' she said experimentally, hoping that Richard would not back off.

'Yes. By eight years.' He flashed her a smile which held a reflection of relief, as if he wanted the subject out in the open, too.

'Does she work?'

'No. The children are very young. Tracy is six. A beautiful little girl. Steven is three and Dana has her hands full with him. He's a hyperactive little terror, very lovable but also very wearing.'

Molly wondered if Steven's hyperactivity had somehow caused a problem in the marriage but she did not want to raise speculation on that point. That was too close to the bone. 'What about your mother? Does she live in Brisbane, too?'

'Yes. She moved up there when Dana had Tracy. She wanted a change anyhow. And she likes it. She was only ever miserable here after Dad left.'

'What do you mean, your Dad left?' It seemed an odd euphemism to use for death.

A wry grimace twisted his mouth and he shifted his gaze to the pool. 'My father had a stupid, middle-age affair with his secretary and got her pregnant. Dad was fifty. Mum was forty-five. The secretary was twenty-five. She came to Mum and poured out a sob story. Anyone could see she was a selfish, grasping bitch who was out for all she could get, but Mum swallowed the story, hook, line and sinker. Pride wouldn't let her listen to Dad and she insisted on a divorce which neither of them really wanted.'

The bitterness in his voice made Molly shiver. No wonder he had been so hostile to her that night of the ballet, imagining her to be another home breaker.

'I was twenty at the time,' he continued, still with the same bleak tone. 'Dana was twelve. It was all one hell of a mess. Dad married the girl out of some misplaced sense of honour. He certainly didn't love her. He died of a heart attack two years later. His wife went back to her family in Perth. I haven't seen her or the child since Dad's funeral. He must be fifteen now. My half-brother.'

He sighed and lifted eyes which were full of sad memories. 'I hate divorce, Molly. It screws everyone up. Particularly kids. I was old enough to understand what was going on but it was bad for Dana. It really shook her sense of securtity. Mum couldn't cope with her emotional outbursts. She was in a continual depression herself. I had to be Dana's support. I was the only one she could lean on and rely on. I tried to give her everything she needed. I was happy for her when she . . . when she got married.'

Richard's gaze slid away from Molly as he hestated over speaking Jeremy's name. She frowned, not sure if it was out of consideration for her or out of distaste for the man his sister had married. Molly wished she had never met Jeremy Lambert. But then she would never have met Richard, and his support for his sister confirmed the quality of his character. She sighed and picked up her cup of coffee. One sip and she grimaced at its coldness.

'Want a fresh cup?' Richard immediately offered.

'No thanks.' She smiled and he smiled back, and her heart lifted with relief. Jeremy had been shrugged off.

'If you're really interested in my family, I could show you a chart of my paternal line going right back to the fifteenth century,' he said with the familiar, teasing lilt.

'You're kidding.'

'Nope. Even got a sixteenth-century ancestor called Neptune Blood.'

'Now I know you're kidding. No one could have such a name.'

'Absolute truth, I swear.'

She still looked sceptical. 'Was he a pirate?'

Richard's eyes danced at her. 'He was a clergyman. You see? I come from a long line of holy men.'

She laughed. 'Even holy thieves. Is your convict on this chart, too?'

'Of course. A very necessary link.'

She was beginning to believe him. 'Did you do all the research on your lineage?'

'The Australian part, but I had to get some help from an English genealogist to go right back. I found it a very interesting challenge. Fascinating really. To me, anyway,' he added diffidently.

'It sounds fascinating. I'd like to see this chart,' she declared eagerly.

'Do you feel like moving? It's upstairs in the study.'

Upstairs. But that didn't worry her any more. 'Let's go,' she said, swinging her legs off the lounger and standing up in readiness.

He bounded up and took her hand. 'Have you read Jane Austen's *Pride and Prejudice*?'

'Yes. But what's that got to do with your family tree?'

His face was lit by the triumphant glee of a hobby enthusiast who has found an enthusiastic listener.

'Remember Lady Catherine de Bourgh?'

She nodded, still looking quizzical. 'Mr Collins's patroness and the formidable aunt,' she recited in confirmation.

'Well, I reckon Jane Austen picked up that name from a real person because . . .'

'Don't tell me! She's on your chart.'

'Large as life.'

'Any more notables?'

'Mmm. If you count King Charles the First a notable,' he said airily.

'Oh boy! Thieves, clergymen, fictional characters and royalty. This I've got to see!' She ran up the stairs ahead of him and paused on the landing, not knowing which way to turn.

'Door on the right,' he said helpfully.

She pushed it open and found herself in a fascinating room. In its centre stood a magnificent cedar desk with leather and gold inlays. There were french windows opening on to the traditional terrace balcony, but all the rest of the wall space was taken up with chests of drawers and bookcases reaching to the ceiling.

'Some study!' she exclaimed. On impulse she

circled the desk, dropped into the studded leather armchair behind it, swivelling it around in delight. 'You must feel like a king pin in this room, never mind your noble ancestors.'

Richard laughed at her exuberance and crossed to a deep chest of drawers. He opened one and took out a large chart which he then spread on the desk in front of her. 'Cast your eyes over that, you unbeliever.'

Molly was immediately intrigued by the meticulous documentation in front of her. Richard moved around to stand at her shoulder and point out the names to which he had laid claim. He told her fascinating stories about various branches of his family and Molly listened and questioned and was tremendously impressed by all the information he had acquired in his research.

'I must be boring you,' he said after they had pored over the chart for quite some time.

'No, you're not,' she insisted, turning her face up to him, her eyes glowing with interest. 'I love hearing stories about old times.'

He smiled his pleasure at her enthusiasm and the hand closest to Molly lifted and caressed her cheek. Reacting instinctively to the gentle touch her face leaned against his palm, and suddenly the smile was gone and the look in his eyes scorched her soul.

'I love you,' he said softly and there was a wealth of feeling in the words.

'Oh, Richard,' she breathed, her heart swelling with love for him.

Then she was in his arms and he was kissing

her with a feverish hunger which she fed with a voracious hunger of her own, exulting in the knowledge that he loved her. She loved him, and she could not have enough of him and his loving. Her hands explored the contours of his body as possessively as his covered hers, clutching, moulding, grinding closer in their need to be one.

Richard's fingers dug under the elastic support of her bikini pants, closed over the rounded flesh there and thrust her hard against him, blindly seeking an appeasement for his own arousal. Yes, yes, Molly thought fiercely, driven to yield to him by the melting heat of her own desire.

Richard suddenly tore his mouth from hers and leaned his head on her forehead, breathing harshly. 'Molly . . .' the name was a hoarse plea, '. . . stop me now if you want to.' The words carried unbearable strain.

'I don't want you to stop,' she whispered, loving him all the more for his deference to her needs.

There was a sharply indrawn breath. His hands snapped up and thrust through her hair, roughly pulling her head back. His eyes glittered down at her, need desperate to confirm need. 'Do you mean it?'

'Love me,' she begged in urgent reply.

'Love you! My God!'

In a whirlwind of movement he swung her off her feet and was off, out of the study, across the landing, kicking a door open, throwing aside a quilted cover and lowering her on to a wide bed. In a matter of moments he was naked and so was she and their bodies were savouring the sense of touch with a wild compulsion which knew no taboos.

They were drunk with their erotic play, driven by the intoxicant of claiming all that had been most desired, and when there was only the ultimate act of possession left unfulfilled, only then did they give themselves to it, wholly, in ecstatic unison, surrendering to each other in a rhythm as old as time itself, the pulse of life, of giving and receiving and creating something new and wonderful and theirs to cherish forever.

When all passion had been overwhelmingly sated, they lay entwined in the languorous aftermath of their mating and their oneness lingered on in their hearts and minds, a pulsing of beautiful harmony, the peace of total fulfilment. They said nothing. Words could not have expressed their utter contentment. The soft caress of fingertips played a muted echo of the exquisite tune their bodies had composed.

The door-chimes seemed distant, unimportant, irrelevant, not of their world. But they kept on and on, determined on intrusion. Molly lifted her head from its nestled place on Richard's chest. He gently pressed it down again.

'Whoever it is can go away,' he murmured.

The door-chimes stopped pealing. Silence, their own blissful silence, enclosed them once more like a blanket of security that nothing could pierce. Molly sighed with pleasure and snuggled a little closer. Richard stroked her hair with loving tenderness. Then came the unmistakable noise of a door being opened and closed. Tension swept into their bodies with each clack of high-heels on the slate below.

'Richard? Are you up there?' A strained, urgent cry.

'Dana?' Incredulity and concern made the name a strangled sound.

'Richard?' Louder. Desperate.

'Is that you, Dana?' Still disbelief but Richard was moving, drawn into reaction.

'Oh, thank God you're home!' Deep relief. Then quick purpose. 'I'm coming up.'

'No!' Sharp command. 'Stay there! I'll be right down. Go and make yourself some coffee or something,' he added distractedly, his eyes frantically apologising to Molly as he lifted her aside. 'Stay here,' he whispered.

'It's your sister?' she whispered back, an ominous fear creeping into her heart.

He nodded, anxiety sharpening his eyes. 'Something must be wrong. She wouldn't come like this otherwise. I'll have to talk to her, Molly.' It was a plea for understanding.

Then he was gone, swiftly, sharply, turning his back on her and disappearing through a doorway Molly had not even noticed. Water splashing indicated he was taking a quick shower. Of course there would have to be an *en suite* bathroom, Molly thought, denying entry to more panicky thoughts. Richard would not be running downstairs every time he wanted to wash. And a dressing room. There was no wardrobe or chest of drawers for his clothes that she could see. There was only the bed and twin bedside tables and an armchair.

The water stopped running. Molly heard the

rustle of clothes. She felt conspicuously naked. A shiver ran over her skin. She pulled herself up to a sitting position and hugged Richard's pillow to her, retaining the warmth where his head had lain. It made her feel less lonely, less abandoned, but it did not take the chill of fear from her heart and the panic crowding into her mind.

Why had Dana come? All the way from Brisbane on an unannounced visit. She had come flying down here to Richard, the brother she had leaned on, relied on for emotional support. And she had come alone. Without her husband. Where was Jeremy? Why had Dana come without him?

Oh dear Lord! Please ... please don't let anything come between Richard and me, Molly cried from the depths of her soul.

CHAPTER TEN

RICHARD reappeared, clothed in jeans and pulling on a casual knit shirt. The torment in his eyes was a reflection of hers. He sat on the bed and took hold of her upper arms in a reassuring grip.

'I'm sorry. I have to go and talk to her. Maybe it's nothing serious.'

Molly shook her head. 'Richard, I can't stay here like this. Please bring me my clothes and bag from the changing room downstairs. You can't just fob off your sister when she's come all this way to see you. You can call me a taxi and I'll go home.'

'I don't want you to go home. Wait and see,' he pleaded softly.

'No. It won't do. You know it won't.'

He heaved a sigh and gathered her into his arms, pillow and all. 'Did she have to come today?' he breathed in savage frustration.

'Will you come to my home later? When Dana's gone?' Molly whispered urgently, needing that assurance to quell the fear which was twisting her stomach.

'As soon as I can,' he promised, and when he pulled away the look in his eyes expressed a need as great as hers. 'I'll bring up your clothes in a few minutes. I'll have to explain to Dana. You understand?' he added anxiously.

Her cheeks flamed at the thought of their

intimacy being so exposed but there was no alternative. 'Yes. Yes. Go on,' she said in an agonised rush.

He pressed a fervent kiss on her forehead and strode swiftly from the room. She listened to his footsteps on the stairs, each one adding an oppressive weight to her heart as he moved away from her and towards his sister.

In a bid to shake off the dread which had crawled over her peace of mind, Molly tossed away the pillow and pushed herself off the bed, impelled towards positive action. If she was to dress and meet Richard's sister, however briefly, pride demanded that she look presentable.

Her surmise about the *en suite* bathroom and dressing room proved correct. Molly gave herself a brisk shower, borrowed a bathrobe which was hanging on a nearby peg, then raided the shaving cabinet for a comb. She tidied the unruly red-gold tresses as best she could then returned to the bedroom.

Richard had not come back, yet he had been gone for at least a quarter of an hour. Molly sat on the bed and could not stop herself from fretting over what was being said downstairs. Each minute increased her stress. Her nerves were in shreds when at last she heard footsteps climbing the stairs. She jumped off the bed, then rocked from one foot to the other in an agony of uncertainty.

The bedroom door opened. Richard filled its space, her skirt and tunic top hanging over one arm, her bag in his other hand. He paused there, the grey eyes shooting over Molly with sharp intensity. Then he seemed to withdraw inside himself, mouth tightening into a thin line, eyes shuttered, his whole face as expressionless as stone.

The need to break through the impassive mask drove Molly forward. She took the bag and clothes, her eyes silently begging him for an explanation. She was too frightened to ask out loud. He drew in a deep breath and sighed. The action softened his face but it took on tired lines and there was a sick weariness in his eyes.

'I'm sorry I was so long,' he murmured. 'It's best that you get dressed and go, Molly.'

'What is it?' she croaked, trying to speak over the lump in her throat and frantic to know what had wrought this change in him.

He hesitated, his eyes evading hers. 'It's a personal matter. A family problem. It'll take some time to sort it out. It's best that you go,' he repeated insistently.

With a heavy heart Molly turned back towards the bed. She slipped her arms out of the bathrobe and began to dress, conscious of Richard's gaze fixed on her. It was a hungry gaze but it did not hold the warmth of desire. It made Molly's skin prickle with alarm. Something was terribly wrong and it was making Richard view her differently. She fitted the green sandals on to her feet and stuffed the discarded bikini into her bag.

'I'm ready,' she stated, her voice shaking with the turmoil of her emotions.

He came to her then, wrapping her in iron-tight arms and kissing her with a kind of angry desperation which spoke of uncertainty where there had been no uncertainty before. 'What we had together . . .' His voice was an urgent rasp in her ear. '. . . You did want it? You wanted me?'

She jerked her head back. The searing doubt in his eyes choked her. How could he doubt? 'Yes. Yes,' she forced out vehemently.

The doubt receded and determination took its place. 'I'll work it out somehow,' he muttered grimly. 'Come and meet Dana. I know it's embarrassing for you but there's no other way to handle it.' Again there was uncertainty in his eyes. 'You don't mind too much, do you, Molly?'

'No,' she said with a steadiness she did not feel. 'As you say, it can't be helped, and she is your sister.'

Richard tucked her tightly to his side as if needing the confirmation of their closeness, physically as well as mentally. They walked downstairs together.

Dana was sitting at the dining-table, her head in her hands, an untouched cup of coffee in front of her. The pose stamped a sharp image of Beth on Molly's memory. Her friend had sat in similar dejection last week, and the image was even more sharply emphasised when Dana lifted a tear-stained face.

'Dana, this is Molly Fitzgerald. Molly, my sister, Dana,' Richard announced rather formally.

Molly waited but Richard's sister said nothing. In fact her eyes weren't quite focused on Molly's face, yet they were looking at her. Molly's unease moved up a notch.

'Hallo, Dana,' she forced out, too discomfited by the blank stare to wait for the other woman's acknowledgment of the introduction.

Dana gave a slight shake of the head as if recollecting herself. 'Hello . . .' One hand moved in agitated appeal. 'I'm sorry . . . sorry for barging in on you. I didn't think. I . . .'

'It's all right,' Molly soothed, anxious to dismiss their joint embarrassment at the situation.

'I'm just going to telephone for a taxi,' Richard put in quickly. 'Sit down, Molly. It might be a while coming.'

He withdrew to the front room and Molly did as she was told, taking the chair at the other end of the table from Dana. Distress needed space in the presence of a stranger and Molly did not want to appear forward, nor did she feel comfortable about being with Jeremy's wife.

Dana was very slim, fragile-looking in comparison to her brother's powerful frame. She had the same thick black hair as Richard, cut into a chic, swirling cap. Her delicate features seemed dominated by the thickly fringed grey eyes, eyes which had resumed their slightly unfocused stare at Molly. It was highly disconcerting. Molly began to fidget with her hair, wondering if it had been mussed by Richard's last embrace and growing more embarrassed by the moment. She could think of nothing to say.

As if suddenly aware of how rudely she had been staring, Dana dropped her gaze, then flicked an apologetic glance at Molly. 'I'm sorry. It's your hair. It's . . . it's such a striking colour,' she mumbled.

'Thank you,' Molly said stiffly, not knowing if

it was a compliment but at a loss for any suitable words.

'Have . . .' That long pale throat swallowed convulsively and again there was only a flicked glance at Molly. 'Have you known Richard long?'

'Quite a while,' Molly answered vaguely, made all too aware of the circumstances under which she had first met Dana's brother.

'I didn't know he . . . he had anyone.'

Molly blushed to the roots of her remarkable hair.

Dana fluttered apologetically. 'I didn't mean . . . I meant a girlfriend.' She ran a trembling hand over her forehead. 'I can't think straight. Please don't take offence. I've upset Richard as it is.'

Molly wanted to ask why she had come but Dana's eyes had filled with tears again and it was too personal a question anyway. Richard was the person to ask, but he had withheld a specific answer. The situation was making Molly sick with tension.

Richard's reappearance brought a little relief. 'Taxi should be here in ten minutes or so. Would you like a drink, Molly?'

'Yes, please,' she said gratefully.

'Hot or cold? There's fresh coffee in the percolator.'

'Coffee then.'

Richard busied himself behind the kitchen bar. 'What about you, Dana? Another cup?'

'No thanks, Richard.'

'When did you last eat?' he asked tersely.

Dana grimaced. 'I had some breakfast with

Mum this morning. And don't tell me I'll feel better if I eat something because I'd quite likely throw up.'

Richard's mouth thinned with impatience. 'That's just the kind of hysterical nonsense we can do without. Start thinking with your head instead of your stomach.'

Dana glared resentment at him. Richard ignored her, setting a cup of coffee in front of Molly and another for himself as he took a chair between them.

'How do you think it feels, finding out your husband's been unfaithful to you!' Dana burst out angrily.

Molly froze. The blood drained from her face. For one rocky moment she thought she was going to faint. A hand closed tightly over the hand in her lap, holding her steady. Richard's voice cut into her fuzziness.

'Damn you, Dana. I told you to leave it until Molly had gone.'

The door-chimes pealed their musical summons. Bells of doom, Molly thought despairingly. Richard squeezed her hand before letting it go. She could not bring herself to look at him as he stood up. It was the end. She knew it was the end. She would go away in the taxi and Richard would stay with his sister and Jeremy's duplicity would form an impassible barrier to any future for them.

'That must be the cab, Molly,' Richard said sharply.

She closed her eyes. 'Yes,' she managed to force out.

He touched her elbow. Molly stood up but found that her legs were trembling. 'Go. Go and see. I'm coming,' she urged, leaning against the table to hide her unsteadiness.

Richard hesitated then strode quickly out of the room. Molly steeled herself to look at Dana. 'I'm sorry you've been so hurt. I hope . . . I hope you can forgive your husband. Goodbye, Dana.'

She turned to go, not waiting for a response. She had taken only two steps when Jeremy's voice burst through the house, loud, angry, determined.

'I know she's here so get out of my way, Richard. She's my wife and you can just keep your nose out of it.'

'You're not coming in.' The grated words held equally fierce determination.

There were sounds of a scuffle and heavy breathing. Molly stood rooted to the spot. Dana rose from the table in agitation.

'OK, you're stronger than me. But I'm not going,' Jeremy declared hotly. 'I'll stand on the bloody doorstep and shout through the door if I have to. They're my kids and she's not going to divorce me and you've got no damned right to interfere between man and wife.'

'You should've thought of that before trying a little fling on the side,' was the cutting reply. 'Go to a motel. Ring me at six o'clock. By that time you might both be able to talk rationally, but you'll only make it worse by coming in now. Trust me, Jeremy.'

'No! I know you won't take my side.'

'Stop!'

'She's my wife!'

Jeremyn plunged into the back room, dishevelled and wild-eyed. 'Dana, you can't ...' The shock of seeing Molly silenced him in mid-speech. He stared at her in incredulous horror. 'My God!' he croaked and gulped in air. 'How did you get here?'

Speech was beyond Molly. She stared back at him, stricken by the enormity of the disaster rushing in on her.

'Just shut your bloody mouth, Jeremy!' The vehement command came from Richard as he stepped to Molly's side and put a protective arm around her shoulders.

A peal of hysterical laughter drew all eyes to Dana. It was choked off with an ugly sound of disgust. The grey eyes glittered at Molly as a finger stabbed out in furious accusation.

'It was you!' she shrilled. 'You're the woman, aren't you? The one Jeremy cheated with. And I thought I was crazy for thinking it. But the hair was the same and there aren't too many women with that shade of hair.' Her face twisted with bitter contempt. 'What kind of woman are you? First my husband and now my brother! I bet you'd go to bed with anyone.'

No, Molly screamed in her head but her lips wouldn't move. Somewhere in her mind a defensive little voice was reciting a litany ... This isn't happening ... this isn't happening ...

'You don't know what you're talking about, Dana,' Richard whipped out curtly.

'Don't I? Don't I just?' she spat back, so worked up that her hands flew out in wild gesticulation as the words poured out. 'I'm talking about the red hair she left on Jeremy's suit jacket on his last little visit to Sydney. And the guilt on Jeremy's face when he came in and saw her. She's the one, all right. Ask her! Go on! Ask her! Look at the guilt on her face. You slept in one bed too many today, you promiscuous bitch!'

'That's enough!' Richard barked. 'I know you're upset but I won't tolerate your speaking of Molly like that. Her sense of morality is a damned sight higher than yours, Dana, so hold your bilious tongue until you do know what you're talking about.'

The shock of being put down in favour of the woman she had been reviling, and by her own brother who she had expected to champion her cause, was too bewildering for Dana to comprehend. Her face puckered with hurt. Tears welled into her eyes and spilled over. 'Richard . . . I'm your sister. She's . . . she's . . .'

Her pathetic distress impelled Jeremy forward. 'Of all the women you could choose from, why the hell did you have to go after Molly?' he flung at Richard in bitter resentment.

Dana beat off his apprach with wildly flapping hands. 'Don't you touch me!' she screamed, backing away towards the kitchen bar. 'You men! All you care about is sex!'

'Oh, for God's sake!' Richard muttered in exasperation.

'What about my sake?' Dana fired at him, her voice catching on a sob before she could add pitifully, 'I thought I could count on you, Richard.'

'Oh, Dana,' he sighed. 'Please get a hold on yourself.'

She burst into noisy sobs and covered her face with her hands. Richard breathed a curse and the protective arm dropped from Molly's shoulders. He moved around the table, dismissed Jeremy's step forward with a curt wave and gently pulled Dana into a comforting embrace.

Molly watched him caress the bowed black head and the hope which had been kept alive by Richard's support, wilted and died. Family loyalty had redrawn the lines and Molly was outside. It had been another mirage, her dream of marriage to Richard. He had said he loved her, but other men had told her that. Jeremy. Philippe. But they loved their family more. Molly was just a passing fancy. Richard would not marry her. Not now. There was nothing but pain for her here. She was the thorn in their midst and there was nothing she could do to change that. She turned and walked away.

'Molly!'

She ignored Richard's call and walked faster. He caught her before she could reach the front door and spun her around, fingers digging into the soft flesh of her upper arms.

'Let me go, Richard,' she demanded through clenched teeth, refusing to lift her gaze to his. It would be easier to go if she kept him shut out.

'Molly, you can't leave now, It has to be sorted out,' he pleaded urgently.

'It's not my business.'

He shook her. 'Don't you care enough to put it right?'

'Why should I?'

The fingers dug deeper. 'Do you want their marriage to break up?'

'That's up to them.'

Molly knew she sounded hard and callous but she was very close to breaking up herself and her only self-protection was to hide her desolation behind a non-caring shell. And Richard's concern was for his family, not for her.

'Is it because you still love Jeremy that you don't want to face them?'

Love Jeremy? The brittle shell was pierced through with those words. They stabbed straight to her heart. Love Jeremy? How could Richard even think it, let alone say it? What had he thought this afternoon? She had given him all of herself. Surely he had known that. She looked up into the face she loved, her eyes filled with the pain of loss.

It tightened into grim, angry lines as if she had struck him and the grey eyes grew hard with bitter accusation. 'Where's the woman of honour I met? The woman of fire who would stand up and fight for her good name? You heard what Dana thinks of you. Are you going to let her keep thinking that?'

His voice was a stinging whip, intent on goading. He continued with barely a breath drawn. 'You walk out of here now and you're making a tacit admission. Dana's not going to believe Jeremy. Their marriage will be over. It's up to you, Molly. A woman of honour wouldn't let that happen if she could do anything to stop it.'

The door-chimes pealed.

Richard sucked in a sharp breath and let Molly go. But his eyes held her. They burned into her soul. 'You said you wanted me, Molly. Am I no good to you any more? Didn't today mean anything to you?'

Even that he would use! Molly's heart twisted in agony. He had wielded every emotional weapon at his command to get her to stay. For his sister's sake. Even the promise of himself as a lover. But it wouldn't be the same. Fate had trapped her once again, spinning a malicious web of circumstances which prevented their relationship from ever proceeding to marriage. She did not want to share Richard's bed if she could not share his whole life. It was not enough.

The door-chimes pealed again. It would be the taxi this time. It was out there waiting to take her away. She could not bear to stay any longer. It was only self-destructive to involve herself with people who would inevitably hurt her. She swung towards the door. Her hand was on the door-knob when Richard spoke again.

'I didn't think you'd be so selfish, Molly.'

The cutting indictment sliced through the heavy fog of her despair, and the resentments which had been outweighed by the misery in her heart exploded across her mind. Selfish! Richard wanted to burden her with a conflict which was not hers and not of her making. Dana and Jeremy did not care how deeply they had hurt her. They were consumed by their own egos, blind about anyone but themselves. They were the selfish ones. Damn them. Damn them both! And Richard was just as blind if he could not see that.

A bitter rage crept over the despair. A woman of honour, he had called her. A woman of fire. Well, let the fire fall on those who deserved it! And as for honour, she did not have to prove that. She had never done a dishonourable thing in her life. And Richard's sister could have that rammed down her throat, too.

She tossed her head up and swung around, eyes flashing with hard purpose. Once more the door-chimes pealed and they could very well have been the bugle call to battle. 'Pay the taxi man off,' she ordered peremptorily. 'I'm staying.'

She swept past Richard and waited near the staircase until he had done her bidding. Jeremy and Dana were hurling angry recriminations at each other. Molly listened with a seething anger of her own. Richard touched her shoulder and she shot him a look of fierce contempt.

'Thank you,' he said softly but Molly savagely rejected his gratitude.

'Don't thank me. You won't like what I'm going to say but you can damned well keep out of it, Richard, because you asked this of me and you had no right to do so.'

'You gave me the right this afternoon,' he flashed back at her.

'You know Jeremy put paid to that when he walked in. It's a dead end, Richard. I know it and you know it,' she stated accusingly. Her mouth twisted with bitter mockery. 'But I'll make my farewell speech. Why not? I've got nothing to lose. It's all lost. And hugging my pain to myself is selfish, isn't it? So you can all share it with me.'

She strode into the back room, head high, stiff-backed, her heart pounding with pent-up emotion, her mind sharpened by all the darts of misfortune which had tormented it. Dana and Jeremy stopped arguing and looked at her. Molly snatched the moment and made it hers, the blue eyes biting with her inner rage as her tongue lashed out its first attack.

CHAPTER ELEVEN

'Do you love me, Jeremy?'

He stared at Molly with incredulous eyes. His hands lifted in desperate appeal. 'For God's sake! What game do you think you're playing? This is my life!'

'You said you loved me,' Molly bore on relentlessly.

His face flushed an angry red and his hands sliced a vehement dismissal. 'Words! They were just words!'

'And didn't they mean anything?'

'How could they?' he shouted and turned a frantic gaze to his wife. 'I love Dana. Never anyone but Dana.'

'But you wanted me,' Molly continued, applying the sting of a flicking whip.

Jeremy's throat moved convulsively. The belligerence all deflated and he turned to Molly with sick eyes. 'What are you trying to do to me? It was nothing. You know it was nothing.'

'It wasn't nothing to me, Jeremy. I think it's about time you faced the truth,' Molly said with merciless purpose. 'I had to face it, Jeremy. That night at the ballet.'

'You got your own back then,' he snapped resentfully.

'Oh, no I didn't. All I did then was put a stop to your little adventure into adultery.'

The blood rushed back into his face. 'God damn you! There was no adultery. If you're so keen on the bloody truth, why don't you tell my wife that?'

'All right.' Her eyes mocked him before switching their attention to Dana who was standing against the kitchen bar, her face white and strained. She glared at Molly and the hard, accusing grey eyes drove out the pity which had momentarily stirred in Molly's heart. 'I'll give you the truth, Dana. The whole, unadulterated truth. Do you want that?'

'Yes,' she hissed.

Molly sucked in a deep breath and let her have it, both barrels at point-blank range. 'I met your husband on the last night of my holiday at Surfers' Paradise. He was attending a sales convention . . .'

'So it was then, too!' Dana snarled at Jeremy.

'Nothing happened!' he shouted vehemently.

Her inner rage suddenly burst its tight control and Molly swung on Jeremy, breathing fire. 'Don't call me nothing! Don't ever think of me as nothing again! I am a person with feelings and needs and I won't let you or anyone dismiss me as nothing. What you did hurt your wife, but it hurt me even more, so don't you call it nothing!'

He gaped at her, completely stunned by her attack. Molly was trembling and it took all her will-power to bring herself back under control. She found Dana looking at her with burning resentment.

'Do you think you're the only one with cause for resentment?' Molly shot at her. 'Your husband didn't tell me he was married. As far as I knew he was free to love as he liked. And to get back to the truth, I was sitting at the cocktail bar of the hotel, sipping a sherry before going in to dinner. I saw Jeremy come in. I thought him one of the most handsome men I've ever seen. He caught my stare and I smiled at him. Why not? I was on holiday. Alone. And he was very, very attractive. There was a space near me at the bar. After a slight hesitation he came over.' She paused and switched her gaze to Jeremy. 'Why did you?'

'Why the hell not?' he burst out in hot defiance. 'I find a beautiful woman giving me the eye. What harm was there in a bit of social chat over a drink? I felt flattered, if you must know.' His mouth curled in bitter mockery as he looked at Dana. 'It had been some time since my wife had regarded me with that degree of interest.'

'That's right! Make excuses!' Dana whipped back contemptuously. 'Do you expect me to be still making googly eyes at you after seven years?'

Fierce pride hardened his face. 'A man likes to feel wanted, Dana, just as much as any woman does. When did you last show you wanted me?'

'I've been a good wife!' Dana shouted vehemently. Her eyes flashed hatred at Molly. 'And a faithful one.'

'I didn't sleep with her!' Jeremy bellowed.

'No. He didn't sleep with me.' Molly sliced in, commanding their attention once more. Her eyes viewed them both with contempt. 'Not that Jeremy can claim that as a proof of virtue,' she drawled derisively. 'Because he wanted to. He might have only meant to enjoy a little ego-trip with me at the bar but it was fun. We had dinner together and we danced. The whole evening was marvellous. I loved being with him. And I wanted him, Dana. I wanted him to make love to me . . .'

Richard's sharp intake of breath made her falter for a moment. She was all too aware of him standing just behind her shoulder. So he didn't like what she was saying, Molly thought grimly. He had demanded her help in sorting out the situation and if he didn't like the truth then it was just too damned bad! She hadn't liked it either.

Molly kept her bitter gaze fixed on his sister. 'You see, Dana, I haven't been as lucky as you.'

'Lucky!' Dana scoffed.

Molly gritted her teeth. The rage was threatening to erupt again. 'Yes. Lucky,' she grated out with venom. 'You don't appreciate how lucky you are. How long have you had Jeremy? Since you were nineteen? Twenty? You loved him and he loved you and you were married. That's the recipe for happiness that every girl dreams of. What you make of it after that is up to you.'

The old pain tightened her voice as she continued. 'I met the man I wanted to marry when I was twenty-two. And everything looked beautiful until he confessed that he already had a wife and family.' She sucked in a quick breath and the bleakness of that memory shadowed her eyes. 'I didn't want any man after that. All the years you spent with Jeremy, loving him, having his children, making a home . . . I had nothing but my work and an inner loneliness that craved for what you had. And then I met Jeremy. And he didn't tell him he was married, either.'

The intense desolation caused by that second betrayal of trust was poignantly clear to everyone in the room. The ensuing silence focused on it, tasted it, and the taste was not pleasant. Jeremy started towards Molly, his face flushed with guilt. The blue eyes stabbed him with wintry rejection. He faltered, stopped, made a weak gesture of apology.

'I'm sorry. I didn't realise. I thought . . .'

'That I was a good-time girl?' Molly suggested with a bitterness that silenced him. She sighed to ease the heaviness in her chest and spoke on with dull weariness. 'I wanted you to love me, but I was afraid of making another mistake. I wanted to feel sure that this time it was real and lasting. So I held off, needing to test your sincerity. I could have handled it if you'd left me alone after that night. I even told myself it was too good to be true. Why did you pursue me, Jeremy?'

He shook his head. Too shamefaced to meet her eyes he turned away and stepped over to the window and stood gazing out, his shoulders hunched dejectedly. 'I didn't set out to take it so far, Molly. I got carried away, intoxicated by your response to me. You were like . . . like a fantasy a man has . . . playing Casanova to a beautiful woman . . . a woman he hasn't expected to meet . . . just happening to him one night . . . Out of the ordinary . . . a bit of magic that's not quite real, yet tantalisingly within reach.'

He heaved a sigh and swung slowly around to

face his wife, who was staring at him stony-eyed. 'I suppose a man isn't expected to be vulnerable to romance. Believe it or not, I was glad the next morning that Molly had refused me. I've never been unfaithful to you, Dana, and I didn't really want to be.'

'Then why didn't it stop there?' she bit out accusingly.

Jeremy's hands flew out and clenched into fists just as his jaw clenched in anger. 'Because I came home determined to get our marriage back into the love relationship we should have had, and you weren't there, Dana. No note. No message of any kind. Nothing!'

'You know why!' she hurled at him defensively.

'Oh yes! Steven!' he mocked savagely. 'So he had to have a few stiches in his foot. There were telephones at the hospital, Dana. You could have rung me. But no. You could only think of Steven. And I began to think of Molly. And I thought ... why the hell not! So I phoned her. And she was delighted to hear from me, and there was a warm, beautiful love in her voice, the kind of love I wasn't getting at home. And at that moment, the temptation was too damned inviting to resist.'

The reminder of her response to his call brought a wave of humiliation and Molly drove it back with anger. 'You weren't thinking of me, Jeremy,' she commented acidly. 'Not me as a person. You thought only of yourself.'

He darted a shamed look at her. 'You'd shown you wanted me, Molly. I felt ... justified.'

'Justified.' Her bitter echo mocked his shallow judgment of her.

He shook his head. 'I'm sorry. I didn't mean to hurt you. I know . . .'

'What about me?' Dana demanded with jealous fury. 'I suppose you didn't mean to hurt me, either.'

He sighed and his face dragged into weary lines. 'Dana, I didn't think you cared. When you arrived home from the hospital and I learnt about Steven's accident, I felt really rotten for ringing Molly. If you'd given me anything of yourself in the time before I left for Sydney, I wouldn't have gone on with it.'

'A likely story!' she muttered scornfully.

'Damn you! You're not so bloody perfect!' Jeremy flung back at her. 'I asked you to come out with me for dinner and dancing. You didn't feel like it. I tried to make love to you. You were too tired or not in the mood. I bought you flowers and you said they were a waste of money. Even when I tried to talk to you, you preferred to watch television.'

For the first time colour appeared in Dana's cheeks and her angry gaze wavered and fell. 'I'd had a hard time while you were away and I was fed up with having to do everything on my own. And all you could think of was having sex.'

'Not sex, Dana. I wanted love. The love we used to have,' he said with undeniable longing.

Her chin came up aggressively. 'So you came down here to have it with her,' she sneered.

'Dana!' Richard's voice lashed across the room, harshly commanding. 'You will not speak of Molly in that tone of voice. I won't tolerate it.'

Defiance screamed back at him. 'Just because you were having sex with her . . .'

'Christ!'

The thundered oath silenced Dana. She gaped at Richard as his wrath flew at her.

'Haven't you an ounce of compassion ? Can't you see what this woman's been through?'

Molly flinched as an arm slid around her shoulders and tears pricked her eyes when Richard ignored the reaction and hugged her to the warm support of his body. She felt too weak to resist him but his closeness was a refined torture, reminding her of too many shattered dreams.

'You might think you have grounds for vilifying your husband, but get this, and get this straight, Dana,' Richard said with biting command. 'Molly has my utmost respect and deserves nothing less from you or Jeremy. Regardless of her own needs and desires, the moment I told her that Jeremy was married, she rejected everything he could have offered her.'

'You told her!' The words carried a wild array of emotion. Dana's eyes glittered accusingly at her brother. 'You knew about this?'

'Yes, I knew,' he said in a calmer voice. 'I saw them at the ballet on Jeremy's first night down here and I intervened in what seemed to be an illicit relationship. Because I thought I was defending your marriage, I spoke to Molly with unnecessary cruelty. I hurt her just as you would hurt her now. And she is innocent of doing any wrong to you, Dana.'

His defence only served to deepen the pain in

Molly's heart. Richard spoke more from his sense of justice than from any love he might still feel, and his compassion was much harder to bear than the silence he had maintained up to this point.

'Molly wouldn't take anything or anyone that belonged to someone else,' he continued with quiet authority. 'As for Jeremy, I had a long talk with him and he agreed that he'd been extremely foolish, to say the least, and he promised to do his best to revitalise your marriage.'

Jeremy gave a bark of derision. 'I didn't get a chance! She found a bit of Molly's hair on my suit jacket and all hell broke loose. It's been nag, nag, nag, ever since. Everything I've tried, she's turned around as a proof of my guilt.'

'And you were guilty, too!' Dana pounced with blazing self-righteousness.

'You see!' Jeremy threw up his hands in despair. 'God knows why I bothered following her! We haven't got a marriage any more. She might as well have her divorce.'

'Well, thank you very much,' Dana said with heavy sarcasm. 'At last we agree on something.'

'That's pride speaking, Dana.' Richard's voice was soft but it still carried the stamp of authority. 'You don't want a divorce any more than our mother did. And you know how that affected us all.'

'She was old by then,' Dana retorted petulantly. Her eyes flared at Jeremy. 'I'm young enough to find someone else whom I can trust.'

'You fool!'

The words burst off Molly's tongue, impossible

to contain. The wanton destructiveness of Dana's attitude appalled her. Not only was she throwing away all that Molly would have given anything to have, she was dismissing it contemptuously, as if it had no value at all.

A billowing wave of outrage gathered force, strengthened by the destruction of Molly's hope for a future with Richard. She wanted to shake Dana, slap some sense into her. The impulse was so strong Molly actually stepped away from Richard, her hands outstretched. She slammed them down on the table and leaned forward, speaking with all the vehemence of years of frustration.

'You've lived in your cosy, protected little world for so long, you can't even conceive what it's like out there alone. You think another man is going to fall in your lap and take up where Jeremy left off? Wake up, Dana! They're not around. They're all married or not prepared to marry. Oh, you might get someone who's happy to share your bed. Even offer you a little companionship now and then. But share your life day in and day out . . . Huh!'

Molly tossed her head in derision as she straightened up. Dana's face had the stunned look of a person who had been attacked from a completely unexpected source. Molly gave her no time for recovery.

'Oh, it's a grand life being free and independent! No one to cook for, wash for, answer to . . . and no one to lean on, talk to, or share your problems and your joys. Haven't you tasted the loneliness when Jeremy's been away? Think of having it all the time, Dana. Always having to do everything on your own.'

Dana's stunned look had progressed to a brooding sulkiness under the barrage from Molly. She folded her arms in stubborn defiance, refusing any response.

Molly shook her head. She felt so tired, soul-weary, and she no longer knew what she was fighting for, but the compulsion to go on was rooted in her heart. Love was too important to throw away. Even if saving this marriage was of no advantage to her personally, the need to rescue something good from this mess drove her to embark on a course which was totally foreign to her nature.

Her sigh drew the other girl's gaze and Molly drawled the last challenge. 'Well, Dana, if you're quite sure you don't want Jeremy any more, maybe there's a chance for me.'

That startled her. She flicked a questioning look at Richard, then fixed suspicious eyes on Molly. 'You don't want him. You've got Richard.'

'Your brother?' Molly struggled to ignore the pain. 'Oh no, Dana! Thanks to you the situation has changed. Jeremy was yours when I walked away from him before, but if you're casting him off, then he's free, isn't he?'

'Molly, you can't mean what you're saying,' Richard broke in tersely, the words almost strangled with pent-up feeling.

She swung on him, eyes glittering with bitterness. 'Can't you face the truth, either?'

His hands reached for her but she evaded them, stepping towards Jeremy. 'You asked for this,

Richard,' she reminded him grimly.

'No! Not this!' His eyes pleaded for a denial from her.

She shook her head in mute agony. 'We're finished. Don't pretend it's not so. You know it can't be any good after this.' She stifled a sob and jerked her attention back to Dana, blindly intent on finishing everything. Her voice was rough with unbridled emotion. 'I know Jeremy loves you, Dana. It's been in every word he's spoken this afternoon. But maybe in time he'll forget you and turn to me. After all, he found me attractive enough for a fantasy, I'm sure . . .'

'Molly!' It was an agitated cry of protest from Jeremy.

She swayed towards him, hands lifting in appeal. The words that sprang from her tongue drew their inspiration from the pain he had given her. 'I'm not a fantasy, Jeremy. I'm real. I can give you everything she won't. You like my company . . .'

She slid her hands up to his shoulders. Jeremy stiffened, his whole expression aghast at her manoeuvre. Some demon of revenge prompted Molly's last gambit. 'You wanted me once, Jeremy. Remember how it was between us?'

There was a flurry of footsteps and Molly was violently pushed away.

'You get your hands off my husband!'

Dana's scream of jealous outrage echoed in Molly's ears as she stumbled and crashed into the back door. She slid down to the floor with a thump and looked up to see Dana flinging possessive arms around Jeremy.

'I'm sorry ... I'm sorry. I love you, Jeremy. Truly I do. I don't want a divorce and I'll stop being mean and ...' She babbled on, held in the tight security of Jeremy's eager arms. The estrangement was over.

Molly's shoulders began to shake. The long strain of conflict broke under a wave of hysterical laughter. It was all so horribly absurd ... the home breaker playing home mender, yet still the villainess of the piece, the enemy, the rank outsider. The laughter gurgling from her throat suddenly cracked into a dry sob. Tears welled into her eyes and she bent her head as a huge back-wash of despair rolled over her.

Richard gathered her up, a limp, ragged doll who sagged against him, all energy spent. He soothed her trembling body with his warm strength but he could not reach the chill within. His voice rang out over her head, harsh with pent-up feeling.

'Will you two get out of here? Just take yourselves off! And next time you feel like hurting each other, you make bloody sure there's no innocent person being made to suffer for your own failures.'

'Richard ...' Dana's voice wavered uncertainly.

'For God's sake, go! I don't want you here. All these years I've pandered to your needs, Dana, and never once did you consider that I might have needs which conflicted with yours. Just get out now and leave us alone.' He dragged in a ragged breath and added hoarsely, 'I wish you'd never come. I wish to God you'd never come.'

CHAPTER TWELVE

'Do you want me to take you home, Molly?'

The soft question shattered her numbness. Molly had ceased to think. She had clung on to Richard, mindlessly soaking in his warmth and strength. She did not want to think now. The thoughts that jabbed at her were full of torment.

Dana and Jeremy had gone. There would be no divorce, but the reconciliation had been effected in a way which was as destructive for Molly as a divorce would have been. She had made herself unacceptable within any family circle containing Dana and Jeremy. Richard's question was a polite reminder of that.

Wearily, she lifted her head from his shoulder and drew in a deep breath. 'You want me to go now?' she asked dully.

He sighed and rested his cheek against her hair. 'Molly, I've already asked more of you than I had any right to. The least I can do now is respect your wishes. I should have done so when you wanted to leave before, but I thought . . . well, never mind what I thought.'

No, never mind, Molly echoed miserably. The future of their relationship had been irrevocably altered so she might as well go instead of prolonging the inevitable moment of parting. She sighed and pulled away from him. 'Yes, I guess I'd better go. I'll get my bag.'

She forced herself to walk over to where she had dropped her bag on a dining-chair. When she turned Richard already had the back door open and was waiting by it, his face grim, his eyes so bleak they looked colourless.

'I don't suppose ...' He hesitated and the bleakness gave way to a sick pleading. 'I'd like you to stay with me, Molly.'

Her heart lurched. She quickly dropped her lashes to hide the pain from him. 'You know it wouldn't be any good, Richard.'

His silence was hard to bear. It pulsed with the same conflict which was churning inside her, desire warring against common sense.

'No, I suppose not,' he finally dragged out. 'Foolish of me to ask. Ready to go?'

She nodded and with head lowered so that he could not see the gathering tears, she strode past him briskly and kept on walking. The temptation to give in and accept whatever he was willing to offer was so great that Molly was not sure that honour meant so much to her any more. Her walk was almost a run, an instinctive reaction to the demons attacking her ... the demons that were whispering to turn back and take love at any price, whatever the consequences.

She was in the Porsche, seat-belt strapped on and door locked, before Richard had even entered the garage. He took his seat without a word. Molly kept her gaze determinedly averted and her teeth gritted against any revealing word. It seemed to take an excruciatingly long time for the garage door to open. Richard started the engine and eased the car out into the lane. Again there was a nerve-racking wait until the remote control device closed the door after them. Molly sat in rigid silence and Richard made no attempt to break it.

Molly did not really expect him to. He had too much integrity to pretend there could be any permanent future to their relationship and he would regard her revelation of past hurts as too strong a plea against pursuing the idea of an affair. He would let her go without argument, however painful he found the parting. A man of honour could not do otherwise.

Molly spent the trip home fighting for control, desperately intent on ending it with dignity. She stared out the side window, blinking hard, biting her lips and swallowing the lumps of emotion which threatened to choke her time and time again. The Sunday afternoon traffic was heavy and Richard did nothing to evade it or speed up the trip. He stayed in the slowest stream of cars as if he wanted to postpone the inevitable leave-taking for as long as possible. Yet he remained as silent as she and the atmosphere in the car was thick with tension.

It was even worse when he pulled up outside her house at Artarmon. He switched off the engine and made no move to get out. With trembling fingers Molly unfastened her seat-belt. She could not look at Richard. His stillness was all too eloquent of his reluctance to let her go.

'Molly . . .'

Her hand was already pressing on the door catch when he spoke. She was half-turned away from him and every nerve in her body vibrated to the taut urgency of his voice.

'I want to say . . . I didn't realise how much I was asking of you when I demanded your help in saving Dana's marriage. I was terribly wrong. Blinded by my own feelings. The words are hopelessly inadequate for what you did, but . . . Thank you for giving Dana and Jeremy another chance at happiness.' There was the click of his seat-belt being released, then softly, with sad finality, 'I'll see you to your door.'

She waited until he got out before letting go the breath she had held in so tightly. Her chest ached. Her whole body ached. But only a few more minutes would see an end to this torture of being so near to him and yet so impossibly far from the union which had been made untenable. She pushed her own door open and was on her feet, stiffly erect, before Richard reached her. He shut the door and, with only the lightest grasp on her elbow, accompanied her on to the front porch.

Molly fumbled in her bag for her key, savagely regretting that she had not done so while in the car. The extra moments' delay was dreadful and tears of frustration burnt her eyes, swelling the pool of grief which she was struggling to contain. It was both a relief and a further strain when the front door suddenly opened and Beth and Brendan stepped out, their faces aglow with happiness.

'Molly! I didn't expect you back so early. I've left a note for you in the kitchen. I'm going to the airport with Brendan to see him off.' The blush on Beth's cheeks was testament enough that their parting would be temporary, and the smile she turned on Richard held a welcome which would never have been granted him a week ago. 'This is my husband, Brendan Patterson. Brendan, this is Richard Pembroke, the man I was telling you about,' she added artlessly, but to a pointed effect that made Molly ache even more.

The two men shook hands.

Brendan turned to Molly with a mixture of humility and gratitude in his eyes. 'I'm glad I got the chance before I go of thanking you for standing by Beth, Molly.'

'It worked both ways, Brendan,' she said quickly, sensing he was about to say more and needing to cut him short. Somehow she managed a smile. 'Beth's been like a sister to me, you know, but it's good to see you together again.'

He heaved a thankful sigh. 'And thanks for that too, Molly. Beth told me the letter was your suggestion. I wouldn't have had the courage to face her without it.' He hugged Beth close to him and the look of love that passed between them held a promise that their new beginning was set on solid foundations.

'Well, you'd better be off,' Molly said with forced brightness. 'The traffic is fairly heavy across the city.'

They were too involved with each other to notice that her cheerful façade was straining thin. Beth flashed her a quick enquiry. 'OK if I take your Datsun instead of the van, Molly?'

'You know you're always welcome to it,' she answered matter-of-factly and waved them on, impatient for them to be gone, but trying her utmost not to show it. She did not begrudge them their happiness but the envy in her heart added an extra weight to her burden of pain.

Beth had Brendan. Dana had Jeremy. It had been a grand day of reconciliation all round. She was a dab hand at fixing other people's affairs, Molly thought with bitter irony, but her own . . . She lifted eyes which were full of misery to the man at her side. Her heart cramped at the deep compassion that looked back at her. He knew. He knew all too well what she had been thinking and feeling. And she couldn't bear it.

'Thank you for bringing me home, Richard,' she gabbled defensively and held out a stiff hand. 'Goodbye.' She almost choked on the word and had to lower her lashes to sweep back a film of tears.

Richard took her hand in both of his, imprisoning it as if he did not want to let it go. 'Molly . . . I can't . . . I don't want to say goodbye to you. Isn't it possible that you can forget him?' he asked in open anguish. 'This afternoon I thought . . . Were you thinking of him when we made love? Even then?'

Him? For a moment Molly could not grasp Richard's meaning, then understanding burst across her mind, bringing horror and revulsion. He meant Jeremy. Richard actually believed she loved Jeremy. He thought . . . Oh, dear God, no! How could he? How could he?

'Don't you know I wouldn't do that?' she cried, shaking her head in agonised denial. 'I love you! You! And now I can't have you so go away. Just go away and leave me alone!'

She wrenched her hand from his hold and turned blindly, stumbling over the small step into the hallway in her haste to get inside and shut him out. She did not make it. The door was closed but not by her hand. She was clasped to a heaving chest by iron-tight arms which allowed her little room to struggle. In utter desperation she hit futile hands against strongly muscled shoulders, but it was like beating at an immovable rock and finally she gave up.

'Let me go, Richard,' she begged wearily.

'Not if you meant what you just said, Molly.'

She looked up into eyes which were tortured with doubt. 'What difference does it make?' she asked bitterly.

'It makes all the difference in the world to me,' he asserted, his voice rough with unguarded emotion. 'All this time I've forced myself to wait patiently, hoping you could put him behind you. And today ... today I believed you were finally mine. Until Jeremy turned up.'

He sucked in a sharp breath and his voice shook as he continued. 'And then I found you couldn't bear to face him and Dana. If you loved me, he should have meant nothing to you. But I had to stand by and listen to you pouring out your heart and soul, and turning to him, begging ...' His face twisted with pain. 'How do you think I felt, learning that you would choose him if he was free?'

She stared up at him, appalled at his interpretation of her actions. 'It was only for your sister. To make her see ... I don't love Jeremy. Any feeling I had for him was killed that night at the ballet when you told me he was married.'

'No . . .' He shook his head. 'That's not true, Molly. You know it's not. The expression on your face when you spoke of him at Lee Kwong's. And that first Sunday before we went up to the Blue Mountains. Then not letting me near you. It was because of him. I'm not wrong about that. Even today . . . please . . .' He drew in a steadying breath and his eyes stabbed into hers with burning intensity. '. . . I need to know the truth.'

'I was afraid,' she whispered, unable to deny his appeal.

'Afraid of what?' he demanded, still not understanding and taut with frustration.

Molly swallowed hard to relieve the dryness in her throat. 'I couldn't trust my judgment any more. Not after Jeremy. I'd been such a fool and then to feel so strongly attracted to you . . . I just couldn't handle it, Richard. I was afraid to let you close in case I got hurt again. But today . . .' She groaned and tried to pull away as the disaster of today rushed in on her again.

'What about today?' he rasped, holding her fast.

'Oh, what's the use?' she cried in despair, her eyes grieving even as they accused him of cruel torment. 'You know it won't lead anywhere now, so let me go, Richard. You're not ever going to marry me. I'm forever branded as the "other woman". It's the same story all over again. Family always comes first. I've done what you asked. I've fixed up your damned family for you.

Now please do as I ask because I can't take any more. It's not fair . . .' Her voice broke into a sob and she shook her head in uncontrollable distress. '. . . It's just not fair.'

He let her go, but only to cup her face and gently lift it so that he could once more probe her defences. She had none left. The tear-washed eyes mirrored her suffering heart.

'You come first with me,' he declared with vehement passion. 'Say you'll marry me and you'll be all the family I'll ever need.'

She could not speak. Incredulity held her tongue paralysed even though every instinct clamoured to accept his proposal. Because it was sincere. She could see he really meant it. But her dazed mind could not quite cope with such a contradiction to all her preconceived thoughts.

'Molly, only you can stop me from having you as my wife.'

'Dana?' Doubt forced the name through quivering lips.

His grimace was full of exasperation. 'Much as I love my sister, I don't need her in my life. Even if she could not bring herself to accept you into our family, and I'd be disgusted with her if she can't, then it would be Dana who was unwelcome in my house. Not you, Molly. I'll never let you go. You are necessary to me and I don't want to live without you. Do you understand now?'

Need and desire and love blazed down at her, scorching away every trace of doubt. Molly's soul filled with a joy so vast and overwhelming that it, too, was almost pain.

'Oh, Richard,' she breathed, and the wondrous

glow shimmering through her tears was enough to dispel any barrier of misunderstanding between them.

The next few moments . . . minutes . . . were a whirl of hungry passion, both of them needing to wipe out the terrible uncertainties which had ravaged their hearts and minds.

'How could you think I would turn away from you?' Richard demanded huskily as he pressed feverish kisses around her face.

'How could you think I loved Jeremy?' she groaned in reply.

And their mouths silenced both questions with a fervour which made them meaningless.

'Say you'll marry me,' Richard commanded as he drew breath.

'Yes . . . yes.' The word throbbed with longing.

'Then where in hell's your bedroom, my love?'

A laugh which was half relief, half exultation, broke from Molly's throat as Richard swept her up in his arms. 'Are you going to carry me over the threshold?'

'Every damned threshold there is,' he declared, and the urgent desire in his eyes surged through her own veins.

'Second door on your left.'

And Richard carried out his declared intention to the intense satisfaction of both of them. The inclination to communicate a little less physically only came when they lay in languorous contentment, and then the pleasure of speech was reinforced by the ample proof of their commitment to each other.

'Do you know, I've wanted you like this since the night I first saw you,' Richard mused softly.

Molly laughed, her eyes sparkling a mock reproof at him. 'Even while you condemned me out of hand?'

'Not quite then,' he admitted with a rueful grin.

'When I was tearing strips off you?' she teased.

'Ah! But you did it with such fire! I was somewhat stunned at first, and what you were saying was not exactly palatable, but the way you stood up to me and said it . . . I've never admired a woman so much.'

'Really?'

'You were magnificent! And when you cracked Jeremy across the face, I thought . . . I'd like to have that woman.'

The relish in his voice made Molly gurgle with happiness. 'Well, you've got her to your dying day. And I thought you were magnificent too, when you stood up for me at the Roystens' dinner party.'

He grinned with delight. 'By that time, my darling Molly, I was hopelessly besotted with you. It was a matter of some urgency to win your good opinion.'

She gave him a playful punch. 'You couldn't have been besotted with me. You didn't even know me.'

'I knew all that was important to me,' he insisted. 'And you had me totally entranced from the moment you threatened to spill the soup in Ted Roysten's lap.'

She could not help laughing at the memory.

'See what you're inviting on yourself? One foot wrong, Richard Pembroke, and . . .'

'And I love you,' he said smugly as he propped himself up on one elbow. He ran a caressing finger down her nose and plucked teasingly at her lips. 'And now I want to hear your story. Was it only today that I finally got through to you?'

Her eyes danced mischief at him. 'I don't think I'd better confess. You'll probably throttle me.'

His hand dropped to her throat as he frowned a mock threat at her. 'The truth, woman.'

'When we were leaving Lee Kwong's.'

His eyebrows shot up in astonishment. 'Then?'

'You seemed about to kiss me.'

'I wanted to but you shied away.'

'I shied away because I didn't think a QC was likely to marry a cook.'

'Bloody hell!' He shook his head in wry amusement. 'And here you are, the best damned prosecuting counsel I've heard outside of a courtroom.'

She grinned and reached up to kiss him. 'You can have the courtroom. I'm very happy in a kitchen.'

'Our kitchen,' he murmured, and kissed her back with considerable fervour. 'Say you love me again.'

'I love you.'

'Mmm . . . that does have a splendid ring to it. I hope Brendan's plane is four hours' late.'

And he proceeded to extract the maximum proof of Molly's love with mounting intensity, and Molly did not shy away from giving it. For there was no doubt in her mind that she held in her arms an honourable man, and there could never be any doubt in Richard's mind that he had won himself a woman of honour.

Harlequin Presents

Coming Next Month

Available in April wherever paperback books are sold, or through
Harlequin Reader Service:

In the U.S.
P.O. Box 1397
Buffalo, N.Y.
14240-1397

In Canada
P.O. Box 603
Fort Erie, Ontario
L2A 5X3

ATTRACTIVE, SPACE SAVING BOOK RACK

Display your most prized novels on this handsome and sturdy book rack. The hand-rubbed walnut finish will blend into your library decor with quiet elegance, providing a practical organizer for your favorite hard-or soft-covered books.

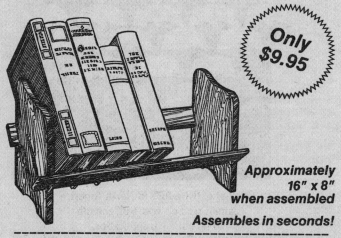

Only $9.95

Approximately 16" x 8" when assembled

Assembles in seconds!

To order, rush your name, address and zip code, along with a check or money order for $10.70* ($9.95 plus 75¢ postage and handling) payable to *Harlequin Reader Service*:

Harlequin Reader Service
Book Rack Offer
901 Fuhrmann Blvd.
P.O. Box 1325
Buffalo, NY 14269-1325

Offer not available in Canada.

BKR-1R

*New York residents add appropriate sales tax.

For the millions who can't read
Give the Gift of Literacy

One out of five adults in North America
cannot read or write well enough
to fill out a job application
or understand the directions on a bottle of medicine.

**You can change all this by joining the fight
against illiteracy.**

For more information write to:
Contact, Box 81826, Lincoln, Neb. 68501
In the United States, call toll free: 800-228-3225

**The only degree you need
is a degree of caring**

LIT—A—1